Death and Sweet Life
One Sorrow, One Bliss
Each One Denied By

The Judas Kiss

Robin Rickards

For Bev.   —sit back
+ Read
        Robin R.

Printed in Victoria, Canada

A cataloguing record for this book that includes the U.S. Library of Congress Classification number, the Library of Congress Call number and the Dewey Decimal cataloguing code is available from the National Library of Canada. The complete cataloguing record can be obtained from the National Library's online database at: www.nlc-bnc.ca/amicus/index-e.html
ISBN: 1-4120-2468-4

TRAFFORD

This book was published *on-demand* in cooperation with Trafford Publishing.
On-demand publishing is a unique process and service of making a book available for retail sale to the public taking advantage of on-demand manufacturing and Internet marketing. **On-demand publishing** includes promotions, retail sales, manufacturing, order fulfilment, accounting and collecting royalties on behalf of the author.

Suite 6E, 2333 Government St., Victoria, B.C. V8T 4P4, CANADA
Phone   250-383-6864   Toll-free 1-888-232-4444 (Canada & US)
Fax   250-383-6804   E-mail   sales@trafford.com
Web site   www.trafford.com TRAFFORD PUBLISHING IS A DIVISION OF TRAFFORD HOLDINGS LTD.
Trafford Catalogue #04-0296   www.trafford.com/robots/04-0296 .html

10   9   8   7   6   5   4   3   2

To My Parents

Chapter One
Whistler, Canada

Dr. Steven del Prado twisted under the smooth bed sheets. The comfort of hotel luxury was totally unrewarding—cold and sterile, superfluous and so unnatural. He turned onto his side and stared through the night's shadow at the seeds he had placed on his nightstand—three red-skinned ovals, so small, so perfect.

Del Prado reached over and grasped the darkest of the three stones. It felt good just to hold it, sense its texture in the palm of his hand, feel its smooth surface against his skin. There was a subtle odor to the seed—comforting and warm, musky and full—the fragrance of Mother Earth.

He stroked the nut across his forehead, over his cheek then caressed it gently with his lower lip. The taste, the subtle aroma reminded him of the garden, his garden—high in the mountains where the air was crisp, thin and clean. It had been weeks since he had left, the three seeds his only keepsake of his newfound paradise—the longest he had ever been away.

Del Prado wanted to go back...He had to go back.

But first, an important meeting at midnight. One or two hours of sleep...He needed to rest.

The doctor fell asleep with the seed next to his skin but his mind continued to plan ahead.

It was cold and still with only the sterile light of the street lamps breaking the night's blackness. Steve del Prado stood alone in the middle of the road, the asphalt swept clean by the afternoon's winds. There was nowhere to go except straight ahead. He could not turn back and the gritty pitch of last week's snowfall that paraded down each side of the street was like a barricade—no one in and no one out.

He began to walk and the words flooded into his head. "The old men...The greedy old men. One of them wants to steal my prize but...Which one? I'll watch my back...I'll watch my back!"

Del Prado turned to look behind but he could see nothing. With each step that he took forwards, the lights extinguished one by one. His gaze fell back onto the road stretching out before him. The gray asphalt had disappeared under a blanket of smooth snow. The darkness became lit with the shimmer of snowflakes, sharp crystals floating down from the black sky.

The flakes grew larger and started to drift across the wide avenue—fat clumps of cottony white flickered and glared like a thousand headlights on a busy highway.

His feet began to drag. The layer of powder at his feet thickened and tugged at his thighs, forcing him to lift each leg high to push forwards through the cold gel. Now, he was running but even his new found youth wasn't enough...Wasn't enough against the morass of white cold that wanted to swallow him whole.

Then he felt the surge—running faster, faster on top of the snow. The blizzard had eased and a single bright light shone at the end of the long roadway. Del Prado pushed ahead and the one light became two, growing larger, growing brighter.

A knot grabbed him in the pit of his stomach then del Prado tried again to turn back but the road behind him had disappeared and the lights ahead grew larger. A face! An old man! An old man at the wheel! Del Prado felt the wind of a noiseless scream leave his lips as the twin beams, mounted onto the frame of a wide black truck slammed into his body and pulled him into the ice.

The scientist sat upright in bed and wiped the cold beads of sweat off his forehead...Sweat?...Or was it ice? One of the old men! One of those bastards! The old bastards! They wanted to kill him!

Del Prado grasped the three seeds and held them to his breast. He would have to change his plan.

Chapter Two
Horstman Hut—Blackcomb Mountain
Two Hours Later

"I would like to welcome everyone to this unique and ever changing part of the world...Because 'unique and ever changing'..." The speaker nodded."...That's what it's all about." The young man stood proud before the three elderly guests, his shoulders spanning the width of the carved wooden podium. Behind him, the broad window gazed down onto the ice and snow of the glacier, its harsh surface turned silvery in the light of the low-lying moon. The logs of the cabin creaked with the cold of the outside world—the mid-winter's bite kept at bay only by the sacrifice of two huge cedar logs twisting into flame at the far end of the room.

The man pulled off his ski jacket. The gray nylon glistened with points of light, reflected off the glow of the fireplace. "My name is Alexander Wade, Dr. del Prado's assistant." He smiled. "You gentlemen must be surprised to see each other, here at the top of the world's best ski hill in the middle of the night...No arguments on the way up?"

Silence.

"You may not like each other but you've all done business together, gone to school together…Competitors in a cut-throat industry. And each of you knows why you are here." Wade nodded. "To see an old friend."

"Cut the shit, Wade." A stout man scowled beneath gray bushy brows. "Where is del Prado? You told me that I would have exclusive partnership rights to this product. He better-"

"That's what you told me and I have your signature on the letter, Wade!" A tall skinny man dressed in a one-piece ski suit stood up and shook a paper at the podium.

The third guest stayed seated, his arms crossed over his paunch, his gray beard scratching the nylon of his jacket, his jaw clenched.

"Dr. Mathew Kardon—Bridge Genomics...Your latest heart medication is America's top seller—brings you in billions."

Wade nodded at the man with the scruffy beard. "Dr. Ralph Hutcheons...Your 'Future's Pharmakinetics'... It's a company that has changed the way we think. Drugs that can make our minds quicker, our brains stronger."

Wade smiled at the skinny man who had slumped back into his chair. "And, Dr. Gerald Goldberg...The world acknowledges you and your company as the first to create the only 'aphrodisiac in a pill'. A drug that will make you feel twenty years younger...For a while." He laughed. "That's perhaps as close as any one has ever got to Dr. del Prado's discovery."

Alex Wade raised his hands above his head. "I am guilty. I admit it! But only guilty of giving each one of you a chance to be in on the drug that will change the world...The first pill in the history of mankind that will alter human evolution, man's destiny!"

"Then where the hell is he?!" Hutcheons slammed his fist down onto the half-log tabletop. "It's dammed cold here and I hate it! And these...These..." He pointed at the two men who sat beside him. "These are not my friends!"

"But the three of you and Dr. del Prado...You studied together—Ph.D.s at Princeton—M.B.A.s at Harvard." Wade smiled. "They called you the four musketeers—pharmaceutical scientist-businessmen who were out to change the world. Everyone thought-"

"They called us five musketeers...So where's Baldock?" Dr. Goldberg pulled off his toque, exposing his vein-tracked naked scalp. "If your plan was to bring together del Prado's classmates then shit!...Where is Gideon Baldock?"

Wade's face turned crimson. He pulled his fingers through his short blond hair and looked down at the podium. "It took me nearly a year to convince each of you to meet with us and...And even then, the product...I had to stretch the truth about the rights, potential patents. I-"

"The truth about the product?" Dr. Kardon glared at the young man. He wagged a crooked finger at Wade and growled in a southern drawl.

"Listen boy! Nobody here likes each other. We're old friends gone bad. That's what competition is all about. Now you say that you dragged me all the way up here, fucked around with who would have what investment rights and...And now you say that the truth about the product is-"

"Very real!" A strong voice echoed from the darkness. The half-light of the dying moon cast the man's shadow towards the three old men. "What Alex said about the product is more real than any one of you could ever imagine."

The figure stepped out into the light and pushed his heavy lock of jet-black hair to the side.

The man stood strong and fit, an imposing frame even next to the athletic build of Alexander Wade. The dark blue of his ski suit stretched across wide shoulders then tucked in at his waist, accentuating his virile shape and muscular build.

A keen brightness shone from his dark eyes, a sparkle of strength, intelligence and youth. He smiled and jutted his square jaw at the old men. "Gideon said that he wasn't interested. That he wouldn't come, that he didn't believe me...He said that he had no interest in us getting together again, said that we were just a bunch of old men who should have retired long ago!...That what I had found was illusion."

The man laughed. "Baldock said that it was just an illusion!...But he'll change his mind." He lifted his arms above his head and laughed again. "So—Goldy, Matt, Ralph... What do you think?"

"What do we think of what?!" Goldberg was on his feet again. "Who-" His voice was strangled by a fit of coughing and a wad of thick phlegm."

"You still smoke, Gerry? After all these years?" The newcomer walked over to Goldberg and patted him on the back.

The old man coughed again then spat out a spoonful of blood-tinged mucous.

"Sit down, Gerry." He sighed and patted the scientist on the back again. "You're going to be seventy-five next Tuesday, right?"

Goldberg nodded. "How the hell would you know that?"

The man in the blue ski suit reached behind the podium and pulled out a bottle of 'Chivas Regal'. "I got you your favorite, Gerry...Happy birthday!"

Goldberg's expression turned from troubled to puzzled then disappeared again in an explosion of phlegm.

The newcomer returned to the podium and brought back two large bottles. "I know it's not your birthday. But this one's for you, Matt." He placed one of the bottles in front of Kardon. "Guinness. The big bottle, the real stuff. I went all the way to Dublin to get it myself!"

"And for you, Ralph...This very expensive Bordeaux... Over twenty years old!"

Hutcheons pushed the wine away. "I can't...I...I don't drink anymore...Not like I used to...Who told you about-"

"Didn't we have a great time together? Those days after the hard work, after we had our papers—our doctorates...Those M.B.A.s were a piece of cake but they were our tickets to-"

Kardon pushed his large frame away from the table and tried to stand up. His weight pulled him back into his seat. "What the hell are you talking about? I want to see him now! Where's del Prado?" He scowled at Wade who was strutting back and forth, watching the show between old friends.

"Right here, buddy!" The man stroked the Bordeaux that sat in front of Hutcheons and spoke softly—almost in a whisper. "Remember the company that we were going to set up, Ralph?"

He smiled. "Do you remember the name that you thought was so cynical it just might work? It was my idea. Just a joke really but-"

Hutcheons stammered. "Vid...Vid...Vidurria Drugs." It was-"

"It was a joke—my joke. But even Gideon thought that the name had a certain flare to it...As long as you had no idea what it meant!" The man in blue chuckled. "Vidurria— colloquial Spanish, Colombian – something like that. It means 'lousy life'...And it wasn't 'Vidurria Drugs', Ralph. It was 'Vidurria Pharmaceuticals'."

Kardon growled. "I've had enough! Don't fuck with me, Wade. I'm old but I can buy you and your boss's shitty little company if you get me mad enough!"

The man in the blue ski suit laughed and strutted back to the front of the room. "I don't think so, Matt."

"It's Dr. Kardon to you, boy." The doctor shook his head and stood up. "I'm leaving...And Wade, tell your fuckin' boss that he'll pay for this...This-"

"Remember the night that girl came over and said she was pregnant, Matt? With your child? Tiffany was her name." The newcomer stroked back his dark hair. "Yeah... That was over forty years ago but I remember it like it was yesterday. Do you?...You made me promise not to tell your wife about that romp in the back seat of my car...Or the abortion clinic."

Kardon froze then dropped back into his chair. "My wife died last year...Don't ...Don't-"

"I'm sorry, Matt." The man shrugged his shoulders. "I just had to show you-"

"He said that he would never tell. Never-"

"Steve del Prado never told anyone...Until now."

The man turned to Hutcheons. "And Ralph, nobody ever questioned you the night that sophomore was killed by the hit-and-run." He shook his head.

"And that was a good thing because you had already lost your driver's license...Too much of the good stuff." He pointed at the bottle of Bordeaux.

Hutcheons pulled the palm of his hand over his rough beard and shook his head. "What you are implying is defamatory no matter how long ago the event took place!"

"So, you finally admit it then?...That it happened?" The newcomer unzipped the top of his jacket and stroked the smooth lines of his muscular neck. "But Steve was the only witness to the events that night. He watched you get out of the car, step right over her body as if it wasn't even there then stumble up to your room. Then it was your roommate, Steve del Prado, who helped you cover up, wash the blood off the bumper, drag the body to the other side of the street...Past the four-hundred block, if I can remember correctly...And I do remember...Everything...Just like it was yesterday."

"And...Dr. Gerald Goldberg." The man in blue shook his head. "I could never understand why you felt you always had to be top of the class. Three perfect scores on consecutive exams...Pretty suspicious, even for you, Goldy. Shit! You were brighter than all of us put together. Even Gideon couldn't touch you academically!"

He laughed. "But your computer hack into the exam pool almost cost you your degree...Remember how we figured that one out?...I do...Like it was yesterday."

Goldberg sputtered and shook his head. "What you claim has no relevance today and...And never happened. Nobody could know that-"

"I could." Steve del Prado grinned. "We're back together, boys. The four musketeers! But with a difference—I'm still one of them!"

He pointed at the three old men. "But you guys are their grandfathers!"

Wade and del Prado laughed.

Gerald Goldberg stood up and shook his fist at the two young men. "You are both imposters. You!" He pointed at Wade. "You dragged the three most successful minds in America's pharmaceutical industry away from their work...And...And you!" He poked a crooked finger at the man who claimed to be their old classmate. "You...You are truly unbelievable. You are-"

"Now wait!" Del Prado placed his hand on the shoulder of his assistant.

"Alex is guilty of only one thing. He's guilty of bringing three greedy old men to Blackcomb Mountain, to give them a chance...One last chance to be part of what the five of us had always searched for. The tool, the pill that would prolong human life to-"

"WE never searched for anything together!" Mathew Kardon pounded his frail fist onto the table. "You are not Steven del Prado. That bastard might have told you some things, some very private things about our pasts but you..."

He pointed a shaking finger at the man in blue. "You are not-"

"I am...Steve del Prado." The man placed both hands on the edge of the podium and glared at the three old men. "Remember ulcers? You three aren't so senile that you can't remember the story about peptic ulcer disease." Del Prado stared at his former classmates then took in deep breath. "For years, medical dogma held that those holes that rotted your gut were caused by stress, too much spicy food, too much booze."

He nodded and stared at Hutcheons. "If that were true, you would have popped a gut thirty years ago, Ralph."

"But then, in the 1990s, an Australian researcher came along. He claimed that eighty percent of ulcer disease was caused by a bacterium called 'helicobacter'. And the world laughed at him." He shook his head. "But that didn't bother the man because he knew that he was right."

Del Prado walked to the front of the log table and stretched his strong hands across its smooth surface. "And to prove to the world that what he said was true, this brave man swallowed a flask full of the bacteria." He nodded. "And the man developed the worst case of ulcer disease that he had ever seen. Then he took a course of antibiotics and his ulcers...Disappeared."

"I suppose you'd call it 'phase one clinical trials'! A limited study group! He used himself as the guinea pig. But that..." Del Prado leaned back and folded his arms across his chest. "That is how a discovery is made. That is how a good pharmaceutical company gets the jump on its competition."

He stood up to his full height and stretched his arms wide. "Do you three old farts know what it feels like to be young?...Do you have any idea?...Can you remember?" Del Prado laughed. "I don't have to remember. I've found what I've been searching for—over a year ago." But I was getting old...Like you three." He shook his head. "And I didn't want to wait for the 'Federal Food and Drug Administration' to drag out their studies before approving the drug for human use. To kill a thousand animals, dissect their body parts and then maybe...Only maybe!...Start on human trials with the hope that years later America would have a drug to keep its citizens alive forever."

"The problems of an aged population—even a healthy one—is not an idea that can be handled by weak-kneed political hacks! And if they could ever arrive at a decision...I'd be long dead...Cold and dead."

A shroud of silence descended on the meeting, broken only by the crackling pain of cedar logs, being consumed in the fire.

"Long dead!" Del Prado chuckled. "Long dead if I had to wait for some government bureaucrat to tell me I could save myself."

Matthew Kardon furrowed his bushy brows and crossed his arms over his chest. "If you are who you say you are then tell me..." He pursed his lips.

"Tell me what happened on my thirty-second birthday. You swore...Steve swore that he would never tell anyone."

Del Prado stroked his chin with the palm of his hand and gazed at the older man. "Are you saying that now you do want me to tell the world why you got so drunk that night? And why the police came over? The gunshots? Is that what you want, Matt?"

"Shit! I don't want you to tell the world!" Kardon stood up and motioned for del Prado to come closer to the three old men. "I want you to tell Gerry and Ralph the reason..." His hands began to shake. "The reason I was so upset...Only one person knows."

The young man stretched his arms over his head and sauntered over to the log table." That's right...Only Steve knows." He pressed his open palms onto the tabletop. "She wasn't worth it, Matt. And I'm damn glad I was there to stop you from pointing the gun at your head before you pulled that trigger."

Kardon braced himself against his chair then eased his heavy frame into his seat.

"You had caught your wife...Married less than six months..." Del Prado shook his head. "You had caught her in bed with another man...On your birthday...Happy birthday, Matt."

"You had arrived home early that evening. Hell! It was your birthday! So why not leave the library early?!" Del Prado stood up and walked across the room. "I guess she assumed that even on your birthday you would still put in a sixteen hour day...The room was dark, you grabbed the gun...But you never did find out who that man was. He was younger than the rest of us, fast—in bed and on his feet!"

"And Matt, even after you got divorced, she wouldn't tell you who that man was, would she? And when I told you years later who I thought it was..." Del Prado turned to face Kardon. "You didn't seem at all surprised because you never really did like that son of a bitch!"

"He wasn't one of us, Steve." Kardon looked down and growled. "He was a smart-assed kid!-"

"He was only nineteen at the time, Matt...Much younger than you or your wife…Still a teenager when he got his doctorate...That would make him -"

"That would make him fifty-two years old and still a failure!" Kardon clenched his jaw. "The bastard never had to work for his marks and..." He smiled. "...And I told him that in the real world, when he finished, he would never make it."

"He did all right. Gid-"

"Gideon Baldock is a failure!" Kardon jumped up from his seat and glared at del Prado. "The bastard runs a two-bit generic drug firm. He makes his living off of other people's ideas!"

"The man...The man never had an original thought in his body and never will! He is a bloodsucker! An entrepreneurial parasite! Baldock-"

"Gideon Baldock is not here." Del Prado held up his hand. "Maybe you're right, Matt. I invited him but Gideon said that what I have discovered is..."He shook his head. "...Is illusion. The man obviously is unable to see a unique opportunity when it stares him in the face."

"But you three." Del Prado smiled and leaned back onto the podium. "You three now have a chance for fame and...Better still, a chance to take back your youth. Just think of it! Three successful businessmen, icons of the pharmaceutical industry—now younger than ever—bring their discovery to the world." He laughed. "If the price is right!"

"And I suppose that is why we're here?" Goldberg spoke in a low, raspy tone. "So that you could tantalize us with innuendoes and conjecture? Hell! Steve del Prado would know that any good businessman needs scientific proof! Some validation that your product has the potential to do what you claim!"

"Phase one clinical trials, Goldy!" Del Prado poked himself in the chest. "What you see is what you can become...What anybody can become." He turned and called out to his assistant. "Alex!"

Wade followed his boss past the three guests, reached down next to the fireplace and lifted up a small nylon backpack. He zipped it open and handed its contents to del Prado.

"One copy for each of my old friends." Del Prado slid three folders in front of his guests then slid a fourth back into the bag. "One more copy for Gideon...In case no one here is interested...Everything that you need to know to make a decision is there...Right there in black and white."

He stepped back and held up a clear plastic bottle in the twinkle of the burning logs. "This is the product, gentlemen...In its crude form." Del Prado popped open the container and tipped three oval objects into his palm.

He fondled the stones with the tips of his fingers. The seeds measured just under half an inch long, their red-brown skin glistening in the glow of the fire. The center of each stone was puckered along its length, creating the appearance of a pair of pursed lips.

"But these pearls are mine." Del Prado smiled. "I take one every six to eight weeks and then...I go back to get some more. But once I..."

He chuckled. "Once we are able to synthesize the active ingredient, the profits are unlimited...Unlimited!" His voice trailed off into the crackle of the burning logs.

Ralph Hutcheons looked up from his folder and stroked his beard. "There's nothing in here about the buy-in, Steve."

"No. Nothing about the buy-in. Just the science behind the seed." Del Prado grinned. "Research and business should be kept separate...Wasn't that your motto, Ralph...Before you became filthy rich?"

"How much, Steve?" Goldberg hawked into a tissue. "Cut the shit and tell us how much you want."

"One billion dollars each, gentlemen." Del Prado spoke in a low tone. "It's a small price to pay for the profits you will see...An even smaller price to pay for immortality!"

Chapter Three

"But now it's late!" Del Prado pushed the seeds back into the bottle and sealed it shut. "And I sense an element of envy...Jealousy—call it what you want—from one of you greedy old men."

He stood up and sealed the stones into the breast pocket of his jacket. "Maybe from all of you...But let me tell you this. You...Even if you could steal a seed—or all three seeds, you would still need to find the mother plant and that..." He raised a gloved finger and threw the backpack onto his shoulder. "That is the information that is worth three billion dollars...Alex!"

"Yes, sir?"

"I'll meet you at the helicopter."

"But Dr. del Prado! The engine's running. We're ready to go." Wade stroked the breast of his ski suit nervously. "And...And there's a storm coming, sir. The snowmobile's faster."

"Forget it!" Wade's boss laughed and grabbed a snowboard tucked away behind a pile of firewood. "I've changed my plans...Safety reasons. I'm ridin' out and if you're not fast enough, I'll beat you to the bottom."

Del Prado cast a quick glance at his guests and let the door fall shut behind him.

He leaned over and strapped his boots tightly onto the snowboard. His right hand drifted over the bulge in his breast pocket and caressed the small bottle through the thickness of his jacket. Just knowing that they were next to his skin...It was almost like smelling them, tasting them.

The purr of an engine pierced the cold air from the other side of the hut. A door slammed followed by the muffled drag of boots on frozen snow.

"Dr. del Prado!" Alex Wade watched the silhouette of his boss glide across the slope, carve a wide turn then disappear over the crest of a dimly lit moonscape. "Change of plans!" He whispered through clenched teeth. "Then I'll change my plans, you bastard!"

Alexander Wade knew the mountain well. There was a cut three hundred yards down from where the meeting had taken place. It was a turn in the slope, a gorge that the glacier had etched into the granite, its blue ice brought to a standstill then forced down hill between two spires of rock. It was the path del Prado would have to take if he wanted to make it to the bottom before the light completely disappeared.

Wade drove his machine over the edge of a precipice then cut the motor as it landed onto the snow, a muffled thud followed by the scrape of the front runners as they dug through the white and hit the blue ice beneath. "Jesus Christ!"

He had been lucky. In mid-air, he had seen the dark shape of the grooming machine, a black snow cat parked at the lower end of the gorge. If he hadn't cut the motor, he and his snowmobile would have slammed into the black behemoth and then...Then it would have been him and not del Prado.

"Idiots!" Wade banged his gloved hand onto the glass of the machine's cabin. "Stupid place to leave a-" Then he looked down.

A deep shadow cut across the slope, an oblique abyss of ice that reached across from behind the towers of rock where the gorge ended and where the glacier once again spread out its arms. The crevasse yawned open eight feet at the surface then narrowed as it sank into the icy black.

Wade turned back and looked up the cut. The moon had begun to sink into the western sky, chased by dark billows that had already started to steal its light with arms of snow-packed cloud. The trail del Prado would take was a zigzag, across the slope from Horstman Hut, through a field of moguls then onto the glacier and into the gorge. And this is where he would die. Wade pulled off his glove and withdrew the revolver from the pocket of his ski suit.

The seconds seemed like minutes and the minutes seemed like hours. Alex Wade crouched next to the grooming machine and cocked his weapon. Silence...Except for the gentle patter of soft snow falling on black steel.

There was a better way. He pushed the gun back into his suit and climbed into the cabin of the groomer.

The machine rumbled and Wade steered it into the narrow exit of the cut. He turned off the motor and waited. From his high perch, he could look down onto the icy slope. In the fading light, he could make out the shadow of a snowboarder—Dr. Steve del Prado, the only one crazy enough to be on the glacier at this time of night and...When he turned into the cut...

"Eat steel, you bastard!" Wade waited until the dark silhouette was less than twenty feet in front of the machine then turned on the headlights.

The silence of the night was pulled apart by the shrill grind of metal edge on ice then a cannonading blast as del Prado's body slammed into the groomer.

Wade jumped out of the machine and knelt next to the dying man. "You think you're young, strong?!...Do ya?!" He tore the pack off his victim's twisted arm and threw it over his own shoulder.

"You see! You see!...It doesn't matter how fit you are, doctor...It doesn't matter how young you feel..."

He chuckled as he pawed at del Prado's body. "Because...If you get hit hard enough...You die!...SHIT!!" Wade's hand slipped into the tear of his victim's jacket and plunged through the hole in his chest. He clenched his jaw and reached in, feeling deep...Searching.

The warm ooze crept up his arm, leaching into the dryness of his ski suit. He groped about in the cavity of his victim's chest, felt the broken edge of the plastic bottle that had held the prize—the three small beans that he would sell.

Pieces of plastic, a shard of broken rib...One small stone. He withdrew his arm and held his find up high against the dying light of the moon. Wade laughed then dropped the seed into the side pocket of the backpack and reached back into the hole. Two more little gems...

His fingers probed the bloody hollow again—ribs, a piece of ski jacket, fragments of bottle and bone then...A jellied mass of...Del Prado's body heaved and the lung swelled in Wade's grasp.

The murderer jumped to his feet then wiped his hands on the snow. One damned seed would be enough! He climbed back into the groomer and started the engine. The snowcat began to move forwards then Wade slammed on the brake and cursed. He pulled out a knife and a small plastic bag from his inside pocket, flicked the blade open then jumped back to the ground.

Del Prado's right arm lay tucked behind his back, his twisted body sprawled next to the tread of the snow groomer.

Wade leaned over and pulled off the glove from his victim's right hand. He slid the sharp edge along the base of del Prado's thumb then pinned the digit against the ice.

With his elbow held straight, Wade pushed on the blade until he felt it strike the hard surface then with a twist, the edge sheared the pulp and the thumb dropped into a pool of red snow.

The murderer grimaced, stabbed his prize and flicked it into the plastic bag. "I shouldn't have to prove that I know what I'm doin'!" Wade climbed back into the groomer and turned on the ignition. The machine whined, pivoted on the ice then edged forwards.

There was a groan, a crackle as del Prado twisted then slipped under the steel treads of the snow cat.

Alex Wade turned in his seat, angled the groomer perpendicular with the crevasse then spat the crushed body of his victim into the abyss.

It took less than ten minutes to cover the five thousand feet of vertical descent to the bottom of the mountain. The snowfall was blinding by the time Wade had reached the lower levels of the hill, the warmer air swelling the flakes into fat wads that glistened in the headlight of his snowmobile—twisted shapes of crushed ping pong balls and wilting flowers.

He turned his machine north, cut across the abandoned stretch where skiers had lined up for the long ascent to the summit then veered right onto the roadway, heading into the woods. Deep among the trees, Wade switched off his headlight and cut the motor. He jumped from his vehicle and waded through the snow to the rendezvous site.

Five minutes into the hike, the space between the trees widened into a small clearing. Less than fifty feet across, the glade was private, hidden and just large enough to allow a helicopter to make a landing. Wade climbed onto the chopper and brushed the snow off the blades—less than twenty-four hours since he had docked the machine and already the winter had started to swallow it up. Where is he? He had said four a.m. Where the hell is he?! He pulled open the door and began to check his instruments.

"You're early, Alex." A voice whispered from the rear seat of the aircraft.

Wade jumped." Jesus, Dr. Baldock! You shouldn't-"

"Shouldn't surprise people like that?" Gideon Baldock laughed. "I'm sure that you gave del Prado more of a surprise than that!....Am I right, Alex?"

"He won't be getting any more surprises, sir." Wade laughed nervously. He reached into his jacket and retrieved the plastic bag. "Check the fingerprints, Dr. Baldock."

The doctor held the amputated thumb in his cold hand for a moment. He could feel its warmth through the plastic – the warm hand of a dead man. He smiled and tipped the contents of the bag into a steaming container he held at his side.

"Oh no, Alex! I know that you wouldn't try to deceive me. It's del Prado I don't trust."

He motioned at the flask. "Liquid nitrogen...Now Steve del Prado is frozen in time. And now Dr. del Prado's own hand – cells from his thumb – will tell me whether his analyses on his own tissue are as good as he says they are."

Wade shrugged. "And...And I got you your copy...A copy of his business proposal."

Baldock switched on a flashlight and scanned the bloodstained papers. "It doesn't say where. It doesn't say where he found the plant, Alex. I need to know-"

"Del Prado wouldn't say!" Wade shook his head. There was a red smear that cursed his cheek. "But I got you a seed!" He held up the small stone he had pulled from his backpack.

Baldock reached forwards but Wade pulled back. "The money first."

The doctor lifted a briefcase off the seat and handed it to the front.

"Five million?"

"Of course." Baldock rolled the seed between his fingers. "Only one seed, Alex?"

"Only one! He only ever carried one with him!" Wade growled and popped open the briefcase.

Baldock shone the light onto Wade's reddened ski suit. The man in the front seat had already bloodied the crisp bills with his dirty hands.

"Don't fondle each note, Alex. It makes it harder to spend if people know its blood money."

Wade half closed his eyes, shadowing them like an anxious cat. The beam of the flashlight reflected back blood-red through the narrow slits. "It's what he deserved, Dr. Baldock. He always thought he was better than everybody else and ever since he grew younger, he thought...He thought that he could never die." He laughed. "Well, Dr. del Prado just found out that it's...It's harder to die young!"

"And where did he go? What did he say about the source of the seed, where he found it?"

Wade shook his head. "I told you that he never said where it came from!" He shrugged. "All he said was that he was going back...That he HAD to go back."

There was a moment of silence then Wade looked up from his money. "But I do know that he found something...In a special garden in England...London, England."

"At 'Kew—the 'Royal Botanic Gardens'?"

Wade nodded. "That's it. He called the place 'Kew'. That's where he started from. He said that he found a specimen at Kew – the only one of its kind – and he took it, stole it." He laughed. "My boss thought it was a great joke. Left them with an empty bottle...And then he disappeared. Del Prado was gone for over eight months."

"Gone to?"

"I told you he never said!" Wade's face tinged an anxious crimson and he pulled the case of money closer. "When he got back he would only talk in riddles whenever I asked him where he found the seeds. A cold place, he said...Cousin of the Amazon. Shit! Even I know that the Amazon is hot!"

Alex Wade turned in his seat. "Listen, Dr. Baldock. If I'm going to make it, I've got to get out of here before the snow gets any worse or-"

"Of course, Alex." Baldock opened the door and stepped out of the aircraft.

"The Royal Botanic Gardens...Very good." He stepped back and watched the helicopter blades begin to spin.

In the shelter of the thicket, Gideon Baldock shielded his eyes from the spit kicked up by the chopper. Once the mechanized storm began to ebb, he lifted his head and smiled. "Have a nice trip, Alex and...Don't spend the money too fast."

Alex Wade pulled his aircraft high above the village, twisted the machine a full half circle then headed south with the full force of his thrusters. Ten minutes into the flight, the snow turned wet then transformed into a sticky paste that sloshed off his windshield. The rain was falling, thick as mud by the time he reached the open water of Howe Sound.

Wade took the chopper higher, the headlight of his aircraft barely able to pierce the wet blackness. His eyes were fixed on the rain, semi-liquid drops that smudged the glass in front of him. It was nearly a minute after it had started that he realized that the smell in the cockpit had changed from musky damp to an acrid sting that seared his nostrils.

He turned and saw the briefcase of money glow, swell, then burst into a blinding flame. The helicopter twisted in mid-air, rolled onto its side and plunged into the icy depths of the ocean.

Chapter Four
Royal Botanic Gardens, Kew—Herbarium
Eight Weeks Later

"Ah! The 'Index Kewensis'...Unquestionably the most important publication ever compiled at Kew." The elderly man smiled at Baldock as he stooped over his shoulder. "THE Index!"

Gideon Baldock stared at the intruder for a moment then said, "Yes. That's why I need to be undisturbed while I study it."

The newcomer cleared his throat and stood up. "Please excuse me Mr..." He glanced at the name tag hanging from Baldock's lapel. "...Dr. Baldock. I have noticed your presence here for the past few weeks and have failed to introduce myself." He held out a broad hand. "Charles Thornton, curator of the Herbarium, here in Hunter House."

Baldock shook his hand but stayed in his chair. "Dr. Gideon Baldock—New-Age Pharma."

"Of course!" Thornton nodded and stroked his thinned white hair. "I do recognize the name now. Generic drugs—American firm?"

Baldock nodded.

"I always make an effort to meet with the visiting researchers but we have so many nowadays here at the Herbarium and at the seed bank." He thrust his chest forwards and straightened his bow tie. "Do you realize, Dr. Baldock, that the famous George Bentham himself, during his many years of research at Kew, sat in that very chair where you are sitting now?"

The doctor pushed away from the oak table and laid his glasses down on the open text of 'The Index'. "George who?" He leaned forwards and stretched out his lower back.

"Too many hours in his chair, doctor!" Thornton adjusted his tie again. "Too much work makes a man old and gray before his time. You need to stretch!"

Baldock stayed seated. "Nothing due to age, Mr. Thornton. Back pain...My back pain anyways, comes from bad luck and bad genes. A bony deformity I was born with that has given me premature arthritis. Nothing that stretching will help. Best in the chair."

"Then you picked a fine one to sit in—Bentham's chair!"

"And who was he?"

"George Bentham was one of the famous men of Kew." Thornton walked to the other side of the table and sat down. "A botanist whose works span the 1880s. A dedicated scientist whose interest in plants was such that he moved his residence to Kew and made the 'Royal Botanic Gardens' his life...There!" He fingered the type on the open page. "The Bentham-Hooker classification system. Devised by Bentham—along with Sir John Hooker—and used ever since, as the principal means of classification for taxonomic research within the Herbarium itself."

Thornton leaned forwards and read the words upside down. "Gingko biloba...Ah! One of many plants we have at Kew—a plant for the brain, for the mind! Is that what you are researching, doctor? A plant to make the mind sharp? Precise? Any luck?"

Baldock crushed his loose notepapers into a ball and pitched the mass at a reed basket that sat beneath an adjacent table. The wad fell short of its mark and bounced off the pedestal leg of the desk. "About as much luck and about as precise as that throw, I'm afraid." He shook his head. "No...No luck."

"Are you looking for a particular specimen or attempting to identify a leaf, a stem, a seed?"

Baldock was silent and clenched his square jaw. He tipped his head, stroked back the strands of gray-blond hair that had fallen across his forehead then reached into the briefcase next to his chair. "I have some photographs." He slid two pictures under the nose of the curator. "One seed I have come to Kew to identify. It's-"

"It's strange." Thornton held the two photographs at arm's length then secured a monocle under his right eyebrow. "Yes...Very strange, indeed."

"It was sent to me by one of my field workers...More information to follow. But he-"

"Field worker for a generic drug firm?" The curator's eyes lifted and his monocle dangled on its tether.

"Please, Mr. Thornton." Baldock held up his hand. "I am telling you this in confidence because-"

"Of course, doctor!"

"Because that is my next big project."

"The seed?" Thornton held up the picture.

"Among others." Baldock nodded. "If things go as planned New-Age Pharma will be expanding into the proprietary drug business. New products, new patents...The product from this seed may be one of them."

"And your field worker?"

Baldock shifted in his seat. "Died in a helicopter crash."

"Oh dear!" The curator shook his head. "The research business—it can be a dangerous affair. I've seen it all before, I'm afraid. A promising new drug can die a thousand deaths—natural, such as in the case of your researcher but also unnatural. I mean the competition. You must also watch out for the competition, sir!"

"Yes." Baldock reached across the desk and gathered up the photographs. "The man had approached me with the idea—looking for a sponsor to finance his research. It was research started here at Kew."

"Of course!"

Baldock held the two pictures, one in each hand. "Nothing you can help me with?"

"But of course I can help you, Dr Baldock." Thornton pulled the pictures back across the table. "That is why I am curator of the Herbarium...Where was he during his explorations? What part of the world did the man explore?"

"South America...A cold part of South America."

"Tierra del Fuego." Thornton pursed his lips. "The southern tip of the Americas."

Baldock shook his head. "I'm not sure. The man...I later discovered that the man was not worthy of the funds I had invested in him. He -"

"Tried to 'rip you off'?...That's how you Americans say it, isn't it?"

"I'm afraid so."

"Scoundrel!

"Basically, then I'm just trying to recuperate my investment. I'm trying to-"

"Where was the accident? The crash? Patagonia?" The curator leaned across the table and stared at the visitor through his single eyeglass.

"In the ocean...Off the Canadian coast. Not where he found the seed." Baldock cupped his chin in his hand. "Never found the wreck." He sighed. "But he did say that the seed came from a cold place—but a place that was the cousin of the Amazon."

"Ah!" The curator smiled and let the monocle drop. "Your man was a knave, indeed!...A riddle! A metaphor! Never trust a man who speaks in metaphor, doctor!"

Baldock shook his head. "I'm afraid I don't understand, Mr. Thornton."

"It's difficult only because the scallywag did not know his genealogy!"

"His-?"

"His genealogy. The rascal should have called it the mother, not the cousin of the Amazon." Thornton's face creased back into a triumphant grin. "You see, sir, there are only three places on this earth that are cold—the far north, the far south or..." He pointed into the air. "Up."

"Up?"

"Up! Look at the seed, doctor." The curator fingered one of the photos. "Look at the husk, thick like a walnut. And the scratch here, along the stone's edge." He pointed at a thin yellow line where the red-brown of the nut had been broken. "A fatty layer—nutrition but also insulation."

He tapped the picture with the yellowed nail of his forefinger. "Your specimen originated from altitude. The mother of the mighty Amazon River." He laughed. "The high mountains of the eastern Andes!"

"Great. That narrows it down to three or four countries and two or three thousand miles of bad hiking."

"This is progress, sir!" Thornton stuffed his monocle into the breast pocket of his jacket and smiled. "My job as curator is done. Now!...I shall refer you on to the expert!"

Baldock laughed. "After all these weeks, Mr. Thornton. After all these weeks of poring through these books." He pointed at the volumes stacked into the shelves behind him. "AND the 'Index Kewensis'. I should have come to you first. I-"

"My fault, doctor." Thornton stood up and held out his hand. "It is my responsibility to meet everyone who passes through these hallowed halls but with the new wave in pharmaceutical science, herbalism...Call it what you will." He shook his head. "I have been flooded—at least one new researcher every day!"

"But now you will get personalized attention. I assure you." The curator pulled at his bow tie. "I shall arrange it for tomorrow morning—nine a.m. At precisely this spot." He tapped on the table. "And I shall bring a man who will be as anxious to meet you, Dr. Baldock, as you him."

"One of our finest research fellows, nearing the end of his Sir Joseph Banks Scholarship for the study of our 'Economic Botany Collections'. A very talented young man." He puffed out his chest like a proud peacock. "An excellent researcher and a talented artist. We have had him draw for the collections ever since he arrived...Mr. Diego Crantz."

Chapter Five

The young man had arrived early. He alternated between sitting and standing, shifting in his chair then pacing the tile next to the table where George Bentham had done his work. Finally, he sat back down and scribbled a line of nervous prose and drew a shadow of a tall palm – reassurance for himself, for his career. He shook his head, crumpled the single page then pitched it into the waste bin. In less than two months his time at Kew would be over and no job offers—not in the field that he wanted.

Professor Thornton had been as excited to tell him as he had been to hear the news. Dr. Baldock...Dr. Gideon Baldock of New-Age Pharma here, at Kew Gardens! Expansion of the business, searching for a proprietary product, a plant source, reliable help required! And the plant? Unknown but likely originating from the part of the world that Diego Crantz knew best.

The young man sat down and smoothed back his curly, blond hair. His hands were shaking. God! A man could study all his life, know his profession better than he could know his own soul and it still all comes down to selling yourself! Bluster and bluff!

A job interview or a chance meeting—the successful job candidate should always be ready, just in case.

He sighed. "Shit! I wish Thornton hadn't told me who he was!"

"Mr. Crantz?" A sharp voice sounded directly behind him.

The young man jumped to his feet and sent his chair crashing onto its side. "Yes! Mr..." He looked at the newcomer's name tag. "Dr. Baldock. I've heard...I've heard great things about your company. I..." He held out a sweaty hand. "Diego Crantz—B.Sc., biology at U. of Southern California—Irvine, Masters in Ethnobotany at Reading, here in the U.K. I... Currently, I'm a fellow here at Kew on a Sir Joseph Banks Scholarship. And I draw pictures of the specimens – seeds, plants. Drawings are much more informative than photographs." He nodded. "And I study the 'Economic Botany Collections' with the goal of-"

"Interesting—that was my next course of action in my search. To view the 'Economic Botany Collections'."

"Yes, sir." Crantz clenched his hands and pulled his necktie tight. The purposeful action forced the tremor from his hands. He leaned back against the table and crossed his arms over his chest.

"Our collection was started by Sir William Hooker in the mid-1800s. It was established, as Sir William said to 'render great service to the merchant, the manufacturer, the physician, the chemist, the druggist, the dyer, the carpenter, and the cabinet-maker and artisans of every description, who might here find the raw materials employed in their several professions correctly named'." He smiled, revealing a set of perfect teeth. "And the collection grows more important by the day, with all the interest in plant medicines, new herbal remedies and-"

"Where are you from, Diego?" Baldock sat down at Bentham's table and pulled the two photographs out of his jacket pocket. "You're American."

"From Seattle, sir. I know your company very well, New-Age Drugs."

"New-Age Pharma." Baldock cleared his throat and looked at the 'expert' over his glasses.

The young man's tall, thin frame seemed to shiver in the still air of the Herbarium. Crantz shifted his weight from one leg to the other, the ribs of his corduroy pants rubbing themselves smooth. "Yes. Of course New-Age Pharma. Generic drugs, mostly."

"Generic drugs exclusively." Baldock smiled. "Until now." He showed Crantz the photographs. "Recognize this seed?"

The expert leaned across the desk and took the two pictures. The expression on his face transformed from an uneasy pallor to focused study. The tremor in his hands disappeared and his eyes warmed.

"Nothing that I have ever seen before—not in the collections, certainly not in the Herbarium."

He sat down across from Baldock and pointed at the photograph. "Definitely a cold climate species. The seed size..." He pointed to the ruler at the bottom of the image. "...Would suggest a bush or a small tree—probably under six feet in height."

"Professor Thornton called you 'the expert'." Baldock smiled. "He said that you, more than anyone here at Kew Gardens could help me identify this specimen."

Crantz blushed. "I...I wouldn't call myself an ex-
...My field is phytomedicine research – finding plants that
may be useful as medicines, cures for disease. I have a
specialized interest in botanicals of the high Andes.
That's...That's where I'm from. That area, I mean. I-"

"You said that you were from Seattle."

"I am." The young man nodded. "My parents moved
to Seattle when I was ten...From Paraguay. But I-"

"German?...From Paraguay?"

"Yes." Crantz shifted in his chair. "My grandfather
moved to South America before the war. Not after...Before
the war. People always think that if you're German and from
South America, you must be hiding from something. But my
grandfather—he was running away from the Nazis not with
them...And he changed the spelling from 'K' to 'C'. It's less
harsh...Crantz – C, R, A, N, T, Z."

Baldock nodded. "So, have you been back to South
America since you were ten? Have you found any
interesting specimens?"

"I have been back." Crantz squeezed his hands
together. "But only twice—once with my parents when I was
twelve and the last time six years ago to visit my uncle." He
cleared his throat. "That's how I became interested in the
flora of the mountains."

"Through your uncle?"

"In a way. My Uncle Karl is a mountaineer, a
climber." Crantz smiled. "When I was eighteen, he took me
into the mountains, into the altiplano of Bolivia. It's a
different world up there—the people, the culture, the plants.
An amazing place. Everything is new and ancient at the
same time."

"I used to be quite athletic." The young man shrugged. "Football and basketball in high school but altitude climbing is different than all other sports."

"The cold, the air... Even the light is different. I never made it higher than twelve thousand feet but even that high up we met people—isolated pockets of settlement. People who worked and lived off the land and there were herbalists-"

"Doctors?"

Crantz shook his head. "Traditional healers. Not doctors in the way we understand the term, here in the west. But in the countryside, in the altiplano—it's a poor region. There are no western-style doctors and no drugs that they would be familiar with even if a doctor could get there."

"So the Kallawaya—that's what they're called, these traditional healers—are often the only source of health-care to the poor and the isolated." The botanist stroked the photographs with his finger.

"The Kallawaya have been around since before Inca times. Their practices are South America's equivalent of Chinese traditional medicine. These herbalists were the first to use the dried bark of the cinchona tree—the source of quinine—used for many years to control malaria and other tropical diseases. There's a thistle bush—Colletia spinosissima—the Kallawaya use to treat joint pains as well as anemia and there's-"

"When did you last collect?"

Crantz fell silent. "I haven't. Not yet anyway. I have contacts—through my uncle, mostly and through one of the Kallawaya who my uncle knows. He sends me specimens and I..." He looked down at his cupped hands. "I examine them...But that will be my next trip. I have a number of plants I want to look at more closely, plants with significant potential as sources of new drugs."

"Let me tell you about this specimen, Diego." Baldock took the photographs from the young man and laid them on the table. "My associate...My former associate was able to find the plant that produced this seed but the man cheated-"

"He ripped you off." Crantz nodded. "That's what Professor Thornton told me."

"That's right. And in my business, people who work together must trust one another or else all the work, all the hours of research, months spent hunting for the seed..." He held up the picture. "All those things can be lost and the search must start anew." Baldock nodded.

"That's why I'm here. Kew Gardens is the place my associate first found evidence of the plant. The man came here...Perhaps he talked to you...About two years ago. He found something, something that led him to South America, something that led him to this seed."

"What was your associate's name?"

Baldock hesitated. "Del Prado...Steven del Prado."

Diego shook his head. "I've been a fellow here for nearly three years now and no del Prado has come through here—not through the Herbarium or the Economic Botany Collections."

"Anywhere else he might have looked?"

"This is not a specimen that I recognize, Dr. Baldock. It's unique." Diego fingered the photograph. His eyes smiled with fascination. "There are over four thousand specimens in our 'seed bank' but this..." He shook his head. "Likely an unidentified species."

"But Kew is where del Prado started!" Baldock shook the picture. "And this seed is what he returned with when he discovered the mother plant. There must-"

"Maybe in the 'ice house'!"

Baldock stared at the young man.

"The ice house. It was built in the eighteenth century to store ice from the lake during the summer months...No refrigerators in those days, Dr. Baldock. Today, it's the ancillary seed bank—where Kew Gardens stores any unidentified seeds."

Crantz nodded. "Each of the Sir John Banks fellows takes a jab at the seeds—to see if we can put them in some sort of classification—every few weeks."

"Then take me there."

"Certainly." Diego rose to his feet. "It's a long shot but it's worth a try."

Chapter Six

The cold drizzle began to spit down on the two men as soon as they exited through the white portico of 'Hunter House' and into the cold winter air. Gideon Baldock walked next to the young man whose voice rattled off the wet cobblestone pathway from under his yellow sou'wester rain hat.

"The ice-house...It could very well be the place that your associate found it, Dr. Baldock." Crantz glanced anxiously at his guest. "And if it's from South America, then I'm sure I can be of real help. It's my area of specialty – South America. The botany of the Andes, more precisely. That's why Professor Thornton asked me to assist you today."

"You're not as modest as you were just a few minutes ago." Baldock pulled the collar of his trench coat up over his ears.

Crantz blushed. "Professor Thornton said...He said that I shouldn't be so modest. That no one who works here should be modest. 'Kew Gardens' is the world's premier horticultural exhibit, the only place in the world where so many different varieties of flora are kept and cultivated and...And our seed bank!"

Baldock looked at the young man through narrowed eyes. A drop of cold water fell off the brim of his hat and snaked down his right cheek. "Your seed bank?"

The botanist nodded. "Kew's seed bank is unmatched. If what your friend...Your associate...Friends don't rip you off. If he found...If he found it anywhere, he found it here at 'Kew Gardens'. And I am the one who can find it again!"

Crantz cleared his throat and glanced at his guest. "Phytomedicine is an emerging specialty, Dr. Baldock. A field that can offer more in new drugs than any other field of science. But...But of course you are well aware of that. After all, that's...That's why you have come to Kew!...Mother Nature's pharmacy – no one can improve on that!"

"Watch your step, please." Crantz stopped and scuffed the toe of his rubber boot across the walkway where it crossed another path at a right angle. "It snowed last week and the caretakers let it melt rather than shovel it off the path. It's still icy where there's heavy foot traffic."

He turned to the left and followed the new trail into a small grove of trees. After fifty feet, the path opened up onto moss-covered cobbles leading to a heavy wooden door couched in an alcove embedded in a hillside. The botanist reached under his raincoat and pulled out a set of keys.

"Herb quality is probably the most important aspect when considering a new phytomedical product." Crantz nodded and a stream of water spilled from the brim of his hat. "In my thesis, I have defined three principles for the evaluation of herb quality – firstly, one must identify the correct botanical identity of the raw material...Just make sure that what you have is what you want."

"Secondly, make certain that there are no contaminants, no adulterants in the specimen...Product purity is paramount. And thirdly..." He pointed at the green-patched trail they had just taken. "It gets even more slippery here. The moss grows between the cracks and is naturally oily. If you're not careful-"

Crantz fumbled with his keys then let out a yell as his feet flew out from beneath him and the back of his head hit the wall of the alcove.

Baldock chuckled and pulled his host to his feet. "You mean that if you're not careful, you might fall?"

"Yes...Yes. Thank...Thank you, sir." The botanist bit down on his lower lip and shoved a large key into the lock. He rubbed his head under his yellow hat then pushed open the wide oak door.

A stream of warm, dry air pushed against their cold faces and Crantz stretched his arm into the darkness, flipping a switch that lit the narrow entryway. He rubbed his head again, grimaced then led his guest into the icehouse.

"Thirdly?" Baldock grinned.

The botanist stared at his guest for a moment.

"Your third principle, Diego. Remember? In your thesis – the principles for herb evaluation...Phytomedicine?" Baldock held up three fingers.

"Of course...Strength...Consistent product strength." Crantz sighed and rubbed his head again. "The product should always be predictable and measurable. That implies that a raw product – a seed, for example – cannot be relied upon to provide a predictable result in a standard test population." He nodded. "Consistency...Very important."

The botanist paused then pointed to the streaked cement of the ceiling. "We're directly under a small footpath, today." The concrete had aged, turning a yellowed gray, pocked with fist sized smudges of black and dark brown.

"Leaks used to be a real problem – until the early 1980s. That's when the icehouse was renovated, new lighting installed. Before then, the roof had been planted with evergreens, then a chalk garden."

He shrugged. "Water seeping into an ice storage room didn't seem to be a problem. But for seeds!"

"For seeds?"

"Oh yes! Moisture, even just a slightly humid environment can destroy a seed." The botanist pulled off his rain hat and shook the dripping into a small sink that squatted in the far corner of the entry. "If the temperature's right and there's enough moisture, the specimen might sprout. And if...If the room is too damp, a rot might set in and destroy the specimen completely...Here. Let me take your coat, sir."

Baldock pulled off his trench coat and hat then handed both to the younger man. Cold droplets spilled from his garment and hissed against the electric heater that rimmed the floor of the small room.

Crantz nodded. "Electric heat isn't the most comfortable but it does keep the rooms dry. This way, please." He pushed open a second oak door and led his guest into a rectangular, cement bunker.

In the center of the room, stretched a long wooden table, its grained surface rubbed smooth from the touch of hands and years of use.

A bookcase straddled the doorway they had just passed through, its old wooden arms rising from floor level to the rough corner of the ceiling, its shelves stacked with worn texts and tattered folios of loose papers.

Three walls of the room were shrouded with heavy, clear plastic sheets, each strip just under a foot in width, stretching from the gray cement of the low ceiling to the smooth brown tile of the floor.

"It's a crude dust shield." The botanist tapped the plastic curtain. "Designed it myself. It's a lot like what they use in warehouses to keep food cold but allow easy access to the product."

He pointed at the tinted glass of the cabinets that lined the wall. Thousands of dark amber bottles peered out from their shelter, stacked in rows like tired centurions, each with a label and number and each strapped to a paper scroll. "All the specimens are kept in containers in the cabinets behind the screen. It's-"

"Good! Where are the seeds that were found in the Andes, then?" Baldock stared at the row of glass and wood behind the plastic.

"It's not like that, sir." Crantz shook his head, apologetically. "These are the unidentified specimens – the outcasts, if you will. Each container is numbered... They're only numbers. Most of these specimens aren't viable, of course. They would have to be kept in a deep freeze for that. These are the seed samples that nobody has been able to identify." He shrugged. "Or bothered to identify. That's what we do – the John Banks Fellows, I mean. Part of our job is to examine these specimens, match them up to something that is familiar, identify them...If we can."

The botanist shuffled his feet then looked at his guest. "I've identified three seeds this year alone and now- "

"Then how the hell are we supposed to find my specimen!?"

Diego looked down at the floor. "And now, those three seeds are displayed in the Herbarium. It's...It's like finding them a home."

"I am not here to listen to stories about motherless seeds!" Baldock's face turned a deep red. "I have spent weeks here without a sniff of what I am looking for."

"Do you... Do you have any idea of the importance of this specimen?" He had pulled the photograph out of his pocket and held it up in the dim light of the icehouse.

"Diego, you are young and an...An academic. I am a researcher and producer, a man who wants to bring new products to market, new drugs that will cure man's ills, ease his pains, make his life...Make his life more worthwhile. "

"This..." Baldock gently laid the picture down onto the worn wood of the tabletop. "This small seed...I believe...Holds the answer to the most ancient quest of humankind. This seed, Diego, is the product of a plant that, somehow, can alter a man's basic metabolism, change human physiology."

He tapped the photograph with the tip of his finger. "If this is what I believe it to be..." Baldock stopped suddenly.

"Alter basic physiology? Change the way the body works?" Crantz shook his head. "That's not-"

"Not possible?" Baldock smiled. "You're wrong, Diego...That man who I told you about, my associate who turned on me."

"Del Prado...You said that his name was del Prado."

Baldock nodded. "Steve del Prado...I...I trusted him but he...I believe that the man became greedy. I know that he took the seed, administered it to himself somehow and...And it worked, Diego. Steve del Prado, a man twenty years older than me was transformed. He possessed the knowledge of his years but he no longer had to fear the ravages of old age."

A silence fell onto the two men, disturbed only by the gentle hum of the electric heaters.

Crantz picked up the photograph and held it up with a shaking hand. Its glossy surface shimmered then reflected the fluorescence of the ceiling lights into his eyes. He placed it back onto the table. "That would certainly be the...It would be the ultimate in phytomedicine. A cure for the ills of old age...It would transform the human race. It would change medicine, society...It would create a new philosophy about the ways we live."

"The ravages of old age…It's been called the curse of mankind…If that could be changed…" Diego cleared his throat. "When men desire old age, what else do they desire but prolonged infirmity?"

Baldock laughed. "St. Augustine – Bishop of Hippo, North Africa, fourth century."

Crantz smiled. "Yes. St. Augustine."

"Then you know how important it is to identify this seed?"

The botanist nodded. "Maybe in the visitor's book. Every researcher, everyone who comes in here has to register. If we can find your associate's name, it may show us what seeds he examined."

Chapter Seven

Crantz stepped over to the bookcase and reached to the top shelf. He pulled three large tomes away from their perch and thumped them down onto the tabletop. He turned back and grasped a binder from the empty space then opened it flat next to the three volumes he had just removed.

The two men sat down and began to peruse the pages.

"Your associate—he was here about a year ago?" Crantz flipped through the sheets of paper then fumbled with his hand in the breast pocket of his shirt.

"At least one year ago. Perhaps closer to two years." Baldock cleared his throat. "I...I don't believe that he ever told me when he had first made his discovery...Just that he had found it here, at Kew."

"Damn! I can't find my-" Crantz shook his head and laughed.

"Can't find what?"

"My glasses." The botanist turned a page and chuckled. "My glasses that I don't need! I had eye surgery about six weeks ago. Laser cuts in the cornea so that my near vision improves. Works great! I just keep on forgetting that I don't need glasses anymore!" He scanned the small print. "And his name was del..."

"Del Prado. Dr. Steven del Prado." Baldock looked over the botanist's shoulder. "Sometimes he just wrote it as d. Prado."

Diego Crantz thumbed the columns of names and numbers. On the far left was a scrawl of signatures – English and foreign – next to the date of the researcher's visit to the icehouse. On the same line was the company's name—the firm sponsoring the visiting investigator – followed by another list of numbers. He shook his head. "No del Prado here. Even as far back as three years ago."

"What's this?" Baldock pointed at the list of numbers on the extreme right of the page.

"The numbers of the bottles." The botanist leaned back in his seat and motioned at the cabinets behind the plastic wall. "Each one of the specimens examined corresponds to a number in this registry. Once we find del Prado, we'll know what he looked at. "But..." He shook his head again. "No del Prado here, I'm afraid. Perhaps he used a different name. Nobody checks the registry for names, really. It's more to check on which seeds have been looked at. Maybe the company. 'New Age Pharma'?"

"No. I am 'New Age Pharma', Diego." Baldock's face flushed red. "Del Prado's firm was nothing compared to mine—much smaller than 'New Age Pharma'... 'Optimus'."

" 'Optimus Pharmaceuticals'? I think that was the firm that had-"

"'Optimus Therapeutics'." Baldock scowled. "'Optimus'. There were several lawsuits filed against the company for patent infringement."

Crantz sighed and he ran his finger down the column for sponsoring firm. "Not here. No 'Optimus'."

Gideon Baldock drew in a deep breath and pushed his chair away from the table. "There must be another way! If we worked backwards, looked at the bottles first."

He pointed a finger at his host. "This man, del Prado...Not only did he cheat me, Diego, he also cheated Kew Gardens." He motioned at the wall of amber containers. "One of his employees told me that, when he had found what he was searching for, he wanted to be certain that no one else would be able to follow his discovery. So, Steven del Prado stole that seed – Kew's only seed—from somewhere in Kew's collection." He stretched out his open palms. "All we have to do is find an empty bottle and the information that goes along with it."

"Impossible." The botanist shook his head. "There are thousands of containers here in the ice house, each one too dark to see its contents from the outside. Going through each one, opening up hundreds, maybe thousands before we find one that is empty..."

He sighed. "And even if we found one empty bottle, how do we know that was the one del Prado looked at. If there is one del Prado who has visited Kew, there are sure to have been many others...Perhaps many empty bottles."

Baldock cupped his chin in his hands and rested his elbows on the tabletop. He looked over at the registry then pulled it away from his host. "Let me check...One thing." He ran his finger down the second column, the list of company names and sponsors. Two-thirds of the way to the bottom of the fourth page, his finger stopped and began to shake. Then Gideon Baldock let out a roar of laughter."

Crantz stared at the line where his guest's finger had stopped. He read the name out loud. "Vid...Vidurria Pharmaceuticals." He shook his head. "Never heard of them." Then he looked at the name and signature next to 'Vidurria'. "Sir Isaac Newton...Shit!"

"It's an old joke, Diego! And a bad one at that!" Baldock slapped the table with the flat of his hand. 'Vidurria'! It was the name del Prado said that he wanted to call his first company – provided nobody knew what the word meant!...Cynical bastard!" He stared at the botanist for a moment. "You speak Spanish?"

"Si!" Crantz pointed at the company name. "Vidurria...It's colloquial, Colombian...'Lousy Life Pharmaceuticals'...'Vida llena de reveses y padecimientos' in standard Spanish – 'Life full of misfortune and suffering'...Not much of a joke."

Baldock counted the numbers in the right hand column. "Sixteen. No more than sixteen bottles to open. That we can do!"

The two researchers gathered the sixteen amber flasks and laid them on the wooden table. The bottles chattered as they stripped off the scroll that was tied to each, their contents dry and dead, the seeds' viability long lost to the ravages of time and imperfect preservation.

Diego Crantz was about to open the first container when Baldock grabbed him by the shoulder and pointed to the last bottle that the younger man had gathered from the shelves. "What are the papers for?"

"A description of the specimen, data about the find." Crantz hesitated. "The scroll is essential to the management of these seeds, to categorize...To identify..."

"No papers with this one!" Baldock grabbed the flask, unscrewed the cap and tipped the contents onto the table. Three gray splinters fluttered into the air then drifted like broken feathers to the cement floor. "An empty bottle!"

He lifted the container over his head and threw it against the oak door.

The amber glass shattered and sprayed its shards like staccato gunfire against the plastic shields. "Bastard!"

"Wait! The originals! We might still have the originals!" Diego jumped to his feet and ran through the pool of broken glass into the small foyer where they had first entered. There was a sharp squeal, a slamming of metal grate then the botanist reappeared into the room, a large steel box cradled under his arm.

Crantz placed the container onto the table then squatted down next to the oak door and began to search through the rubble of glass. After a moment, he rose to his feet, a broad smile on his pale face and held out a sliver of amber, its sticky label still attached. "Bottle number 52. It must be over a hundred years old, sir!"

The botanist opened the steel box and pulled out a yellowed manila folder. "There are some specimens that have only a few words, a small paragraph about the origin of the seed. Some can have three folders this size just for one seed." He shook his head. "Not much in this one, I'm afraid."

He pursed his lips. "This file must have been reviewed by the librarian within the last ten years. The folder is relatively new... Specimens 50 to 55."

The botanist held his breath and opened the folder. "There!" He teased two pages of scrawl out from between the sheets and laid them gently onto the tabletop. It had been written with a shaky grasp, scratched onto the parchment by a failing hand like a last will, a final chance to tell a story, the words blurred and faded.

Gideon Baldock pulled on a pair of spectacles and the two men began to read:

This 18th day of June in the year of our Lord Eighteen Hundred and Sixty-one

From the collection of:

William Jude Gregor

Assistant to Richard Spruce, Yorkshire botanist and explorer

I, William Jude Gregor, leave this one specimen to the Herbarium at Kew Gardens, one seed, my last seed, a seed of warning, a seed of hope. I admit now to the suspicions of my superior, Richard Spruce who had thought me lost in the jungles of Ecuador. My journey to the highlands was indeed fruitful but the bounty of my find I cannot share with any man.

Deep in my soul, I feel the need to return, I MUST return. My life – what little may be left of it – is tied to the mountain and the mother who gave me her seed.

If God takes me back in time, she will heal me and I will take care of her forever and eternity.

Baldock pointed at the vain attempt at poetry. "A riddle or just an old man's try at being poetic?"

"I don't think so, sir…When Richard Spruce went to Ecuador, William Gregor was a young man – eighteen years old, twenty at the most. He was so young when he disappeared that nobody knows much about his history."

He shrugged. "Perhaps he was an aspiring poet. But it seems that he did have an urge to go back...Back to where he found the specimen."

The two men fell silent.

"Gregor left on his own – back to South America in June of 1861." Crantz pointed to the date at the top of the page. "Perhaps only days after he wrote this letter." He lifted the first page and uncovered the second sheet of script.

The wrinkled paper had decayed at the edges, burnt-brown flakes fluttered across the table as the botanist began to separate the top sheet from the bottom. "Poorly cared for. Very poor." He licked his upper lip and teased the two pages apart.

A crude map, sketched with faded black and charcoal gray stared at the two men like a blurred image from a half-forgotten dream. Large letters marked the ovoid shape of 'Lago Titicaca' and two arrows pointed at a smudge to the far northeast of the lake and the words 'Cordillera Apolobamba' and 'Chupiorco'.

Crantz nodded. "It's the same area my uncle used to climb. Some of the highest peaks in all of Bolivia are in this mountain range. 'Chupiorco' is one of the highest – over nineteen thousand feet at the summit, maybe higher. It's-"

Baldock pointed at the words beneath the map and the two men read in silence.

Re: Osculum Judas

Three, perhaps four mother plants, one of them mine... I am hers.

Each mother far apart from her sisters. Each one cared for by her man, her son.

Each son took a life to give his own. Each master keeps her son forever... Forever.

Separated by the peaks of Chupiorco, deep in the high mists of the 'Cordillera Apolobamba'.

The mother of the south cared for by the Indian man.

The mother of the east, by the man from the Lago.

Mine is the mother at the western peak, if she will have me, if she still wants me...If I can return in time.

The last is the master at the northern peak, hidden from the world, protected by

'The Spaniard', a man who goes far back...Far back in time.

The Kallahuaya healers know the mothers. They know these masters well.

They say that the Indian man could no longer endure the centuries of pain. So, he ended his work...And his mother died.

The man from the Lago – he is the easiest to see. Perhaps it is he, the next to be free.

Come to Chajaya and speak to the healers if you need to find me...If she will have me, if she still wants me, if I can return in time.

For the Spaniard man...He will see no one. Until time brings change to him, he stays hidden away with his master at the northern peak...

Ask at Chajaya if it is me you seek.

The text ended with the smeared signature of William Jude Gregor.

Baldock stroked the naked edges of the map. Then he pointed at the title of the script. "Acin...Oscul..." The word had blurred with the years, the remnants of its Latin tail, the only letters that could be recognized.

"It would be highly unusual to name a specimen in this manner." The botanist stared at the faded letters. "In botany, the naming of a seed usually follows specific rules. The flax seed for instance: 'linum usitatissimum' – the most familiar flax or rope, in English. But osculum..." He shook his head. "It must be 'acinum' – Latin for 'seed'. But that would mean that Gregor named the specimen after himself – Jude, his middle name. The seed of Jude."

"A man full of himself, Diego. Just like del Prado, a man who chose the name 'Vidurria' – cynical and egocentric." He tapped his finger on the signature. "William Jude Gregor must have been a very similar man."

"But the words. The...The poetry—if you can call it poetry…..Metaphor, perhaps. 'Mine is the mother at the western peak. If she will have me, if she still wants me'." Crantz looked at Baldock. "Those aren't the words of a man who is self-centered, a man living for himself. I don't -"

"Here." Baldock pointed at a scribble pushed into the bottom right hand corner of the page. "It's the same word again: 'Osculum'...But it's 'Osculum Iudas'...With an 'I'. Can you read the rest, the Latin?"

"It's part Latin – part...Poetry I suppose." Diego squinted at the blurred writing. "The poetry, the English part reads:

My mother gave us three seeds,
The first one for me
She gave me sweet life
But not Angus McPhee.
Only one man she will defend
For all others, life must end."

There was a long pause then Crantz said, "Angus McPhee was one of the men who accompanied Gregor. He never returned. The information surrounding Gregor's excursion into the mountains was scant. McPhee died of some illness – never made it back home."

"What about the rest?"

The botanist mouthed the words then read out the Latin verse:

Mors et Vita Dulca
Luctus et Felicitas
Uterque Deici Per
Osculum Iudas

"The man's Latin was as poor as his poetry, Dr. Baldock."

The two men chuckled.

"But you're right – 'the word is 'osculum', not 'acinum'. And it's not 'J'. There is no such letter in Latin. 'I' replaces 'J'. That would make more sense." Diego nodded.

"Gregor didn't name the seed after himself." He pursed his lips. "But..." He nodded again." But it would be 'Osculum Judas'."

He sighed and whispered the Latin text. "Let me try. It's a rough translation but..." Crantz cleared his throat.

Death and sweet life
One sorrow, one bliss
Each one denied by
The Judas Kiss

Silence.

The electric heaters crackled and then Baldock's foot scraped a shard of glass along the concrete floor. He gently laid the photograph of his only seed next to the old parchment then rolled a smooth, oblong stone onto the tabletop.

The young man's eyes widened and he picked the small object up delicately between two fingers. "You...You have a specimen, Dr. Baldock. You have-"

"Only one." Gideon Baldock grinned.

"May I keep it? Just for a few hours. A day perhaps – to draw, I mean."

Baldock pursed his lips then tucked the seed back into its container. "One seed is not enough. Not something I can risk." He paused. "Don't forget your three principles...identity, purity, strength. We need more than just one seed, Diego." He looked the young man in the eye. Will you help me find the mother plant?"

Crantz stayed silent.

"Do you want to be famous, Diego?" He stared at the young man. "Banting and Best – they discovered insulin. Fleming discovered penicillin. These men, Diego... These men changed medicine. They were the best. They could dance alone at the top of the world."

The two men looked into each other's eyes then Baldock whispered, "Do you, Diego? Do you want to dance alone at the top?... At the top of the world?"

Diego Crantz swallowed hard. "Thank you...Thank you, Dr. Baldock."

Chapter Eight
Four Days Later

Diego Crantz stood up from the table when he saw the older man enter the small coffee shop. He had pinned his eyes on the doorway, nervously sipping his third cup, his hands shaking with anticipation and excitement. He crumpled the napkin he had scratched with his pencil – tropical ferns, exotic grasses – and let it drop to the floor.

"Dr. Baldock! My directions weren't too hard to follow? There aren't many cafes like this one – in this end of the city. I thought that it would be-"

Baldock smiled and shook his head. "No problem at all, Diego! London cabbies can find anything. Even-"

"Did he call?! He should have called you yesterday...Or the day before." Crantz squeezed his hands together.

"I talked to your Uncle Karl last night." Baldock peeled off his coat and hung the wet garment over the back of a chair. He smiled at the waitress. "Coffee, please."

The woman pulled back her ponytail of gray hair and spoke with a thick Scottish accent. "Latte? Cappuccino? Cafe mocha? Diego's American friends always order the mocha."

"Coffee." Baldock sat down and returned the smile. "Just plain coffee for this friend." He turned to Crantz. "Uncle Karl has no concept of time zones. He phoned me at three a.m. Said that he had just finished dinner."

"He said 'yes'?!"

"The man couldn't say anything but 'yes', Diego!" Baldock laughed. "What I promised to pay would make any man come out of retirement for one last climb. And he said that he knew the area, the mountain-"

"And the healers! The Kallahuaya healers! Uncle Karl said to me that he knows the oldest healer in Chajaya, knows him well enough to ask about medicinal plants on Chupiorco – at the top, I mean...Whether there are any plants that high up."

The waitress returned to the table and set a steaming mug in front of the older man.

"On my tab, Abby." Crantz grinned at the older woman.

"And are ye really going to pay this time, James?" The woman chuckled. "Or shall I ring it out of the palms of your poor Mrs. when she comes in next?"

"My poor Mrs. is going to be a rich specialist in less than a year, Abby and then I can come in here and drink as much of your coffee or tea as I like."

"Aye! But then you two will be off for America and I shall never see ye again." Abby nodded. "And ye know what the tea leaves said, James."

"I'll pay before we leave."

She put a warm arm around the younger man and smiled at Baldock. "I'm just joking, you know. I mean...When you leave, I'm going to miss you. And...You'll never be back."

Diego's pale complexion sparked crimson. "Abby...This is Dr. Baldock. He is...We are going on an expedition together. A scientific-"

"Lord be praised, James! You found a job!" The waitress ruffled Diego's curly locks. "You, Dr. Baldock, sir, are a very lucky man. James is the most honest person I have ever met, a sincere, hard working soul and his future is as bright as the stars in the winter sky."

Baldock smiled. "You saw that in the tea leaves?"

"Aye!" Abby answered, a serious look on her ruddy face. "In the tea leaves... That I did. And I know that James will grow old and have a son." She nodded again. "It's a certainty."

"How are you with coffee grounds, Abby?" Baldock swirled the dregs of his warm drink around the bottom of his mug.

"You Americans can laugh but tea leaves are just one way to look into the soul, doctor." She smiled and picked up Baldock's empty cup.

"I'll get ye both another and when you're done your little talk, I'll do better than read your coffee. I'll look into the palm of your hand." Abby pursed her lips. "And it may surprise ye what a man can learn from the lines in his own hand."

Crantz blushed again. "Abby is well meaning, Dr. Baldock – just a little eccentric. She-"

"Maybe she can tell us who we'll meet on Chupiorco!" Baldock opened his hands wide. "The man from the lago? The Indian? The Spaniard?" He laughed. "Maybe old William Jude Gregor did make it back after all and is waiting for us at the western peak!"

"Uncle Karl said that he's never climbed to the top. Nobody that he knows has ever been beyond the first summit – the one on the western side."

Baldock smiled. "They didn't meet an old Scotsman? That's Gregor's peak."

"The Kallahuaya sometimes roam high into the mountains." Diego nodded. "Searching for medicinal plants. But it's rare for anything to grow above eighteen thousand feet. Uncle Karl said that the south side of the Chupiorco is the lowest – just under sixteen thousand at the very top. The western peak is about five hundred feet higher but the trails are easier than at the south."

"The other two..." He shook his head. "The eastern peak collapsed ten years ago. An earthquake must have toppled the highest point and it came down wiping out everything from the top right down to the sixteen thousand foot level and Karl says-"

"Karl says that the northern peak is inaccessible." Baldock interrupted the younger man. "Nearly nineteen thousand feet, no trails—ice and snow as old as the rock – a cold desert at the top of the world."

Crantz nodded. "We'll find something on the eastern or western side, I'm sure. No one has ever been to the northern peak. Not-"

"Except for the Spaniard." Baldock held up his finger. "Remember what Gregor said: 'The last is the master of the northern peak, hidden from the world, protected by 'The Spaniard', a man who goes far back...Far back in time.'

"It should be our last choice. The north is the highest, the hardest climb. It's-"

"I told your Uncle Karl that we would start with the northern peak, Diego." Baldock nodded. "If it's the hardest climb then it is most likely that no one has been there before us."

Diego bit down on his lower lip. "Except for the Spaniard."

Baldock nodded. "We'll look for the Spaniard."

Abby returned with two steaming mugs, tossed her braid over her right shoulder then set the drinks down in front of her guests. The smell of the brew wafted into the air as she reached over to a small stand behind Crantz's seat then placed a small pitcher of thick fluid onto their table.

"It's the thickest cream in the whole United Kingdom." She pointed at the mugs. "And the blackest coffees, too. And when ye've made your plans for the future, it'll be my turn to tell ye what will really happen."

Diego shrugged and pressed his palms together. "She really believes it – her fortune telling, I mean. Abby is-"

"Eccentric, like you said, Diego." Baldock smiled. "Eccentric and persistent... When we're finished...I'll let her have her fun."

There was only one other couple in the small cafe. The young man and woman had ensconced themselves in the darkest corner of the room and had each consumed three large cups of bitter, black fluid all the while their free hands clasped in a loving embrace. The waitress knew when to leave her guests alone and she had determined that three cups of coffee was enough for the amorous duo. The two gentlemen had all that they needed as well.

Abby folded her broad arms across her chest, leaned back against the coffee machine and watched her friend, James and the doctor.

She fixed her gaze on their hands – the older man's, spatulate, curving in at the palm...A man of spirit, adventurous...Restless?

And James' hands – his, she had read four, five, six times now? All for fun. He and his doctor wife had always laughed, never taken it seriously. But she knew his hand – a mix of psychic, philosophic. A hand that belonged to someone who would give his heart only once, compassionate and trusting but all the while an intellectual—at times impractical, at times distracted from the minutiae of life.

She shifted her large frame then began to wipe down the counter, stealing pensive glances at James and his friend. The older man did most of the talking. He used his hands as a sailor would use flags for sending signals. He used his fingers as a soldier would use a bayonet...That worried her. The doctor was a man with his own ideas, his own agenda...A man who knew his goals and pointed all his energies – and the energies of anyone else – towards them.

James sat, as he always did, with his two hands clasped together, his thumbs cocked beneath his chin. He was still young, always learning, always listening—not a man who used many words and certainly not the type who spoke with his hands.

Abby shook her head and turned away from her guests. A cold shudder gripped her shoulders then snaked down her spine. She closed her eyes and, in her mind, she could see the curves and lines on Baldock's palms.

She could feel the texture of his skin – cool, clammy...Non-communicative. And a long forefinger...A Jupiterian.

Yes, definitely a Jupiterian – ego-driven, self-centered. Fingernails long, deep-set, selfish...A very selfish man.

"Abby!"

The waitress shivered and turned towards the voice. It was Crantz.

"Abby! Are you all right? Dr. Baldock and I are done."

She approached the two men and cast her gaze down to the tabletop. "Aye...The bill, then."

Baldock grabbed the piece of paper and held out his hand, silencing the protests of the younger man. "This is now a business expense, Diego."

He turned to the waitress. "Now that my partner and I have made our plans for the future, maybe you can give us a clue about what will really happen. How about it, Abby? Tell us what our future holds – like you said you would."

The waitress shook her head and kept her eyes glued to the table. "I'm sorry, gentlemen. I...I canna-"

"Please Abby." Diego stood up and pulled over a chair from the table next to them and motioned for the waitress to sit down. "You know how much I enjoy what you do."

Abby looked up and stared at her friend. "It don't feel right, James."

"It's just a palm reading, Abby. It's-"

"Naye! I mean...What you two gentlemen plan to do!" She shook her head again. "I don't know what it is – your plans, I mean but...It just don't feel right."

"For Dr. Baldock. A quick one. He leaves for America this evening and I won't be seeing him until we meet again in Bolivia."

"Bolivia?" The waitress pursed her lips and frowned. "Yee're going to South America. Yee're not going back home, then?"

"Not yet. Not until the expedition is successful." Crantz smiled. "Two weeks, maybe three in the mountains and then I come back to finish off at Kew. "He turned to the older man. "Then Dr. Baldock has a job for me to continue on with a world class pharmaceutical company, New-Age Pharma."

"So...We need to know!" He smiled again. "Will it take us two weeks or three? How many months after that will it take for New Age to be heralded as the biggest and the best in the pharmaceutical industry?"

"I...I canna tell ye about the business, James." Abby shook her head. "I can only tell ye generalities."

"Then...Please, Abby. Start with Dr. Baldock." Crantz looked up at the older man. "Have you ever had your palm read, Dr. Baldock?"

"Never."

The waitress reached out and took hold of the doctor's two hands...A cool dampness spread out from the tips of his fingers and passed onto her own smooth palms. She nodded and turned each of her subject's hands palm-side up. "The right hand tells 'what is' – the left, 'what might be'."

She stroked his right palm with the flat of her hand then pointed at the landmarks. "Here, at the base of your thumb, is your life line. This straight one next to it...The line of fate."

Abby stopped and saw the fingernails, long and deep then she pointed at the forefinger. "Ye're a Jupiterian, Dr. Baldock with a very well-developed mound..." She pressed the pad at the base of his finger."

"And that means?"

She looked Baldock in the eye. "It means that ye are a man driven – a leader, perhaps a soldier. And here...A star on Mercury." She pointed to the pad at the base of his small finger. "Dramatic success in business...And here – the lunar mound, at the wrist below Mercury and Upper Mars. The lunar is related to the unconscious."

"And what does my Lunar mound tell you, Abby?"

"The Lunar mound can grow and diminish, just like the moon itself. Its meaning depends on its juxtaposition to the Head line." She brushed her hair to the side. "It could signify great inspiration or...A tendency to lie."

Baldock's fingers flinched then relaxed. "Tell me more about the Mound of Mercury, the business side of me."

"Mercury is the shrewd, active god of merchants, Dr. Baldock." She looked him in the eye. "But also the god of thieves."

There was a moment of silence then Crantz grabbed the waitress' hands. "My turn, Abby. Tell me what the future has in store for me."

"I know your hands like my own. They're serious and warm. Hands that..."She stared at her friend's open palms. "What have ye been doing, James?"

"What do you mean?"

"Your hands. What have ye been doing with your hands? They're not the same." She looked into his eyes with a wide, open stare.

"Where? Show me, then. Tell me how many weeks to reach our goal?"

The waitress stroked Diego's right palm with a trembling hand. "These lines on the outer edge of your palm...It confirms you will be traveling. Aye, but..." She shook her head. "Tassels, feathering... Towards the end of your Life line. There's a potential weakness in your soul, young man."

"And what about 'what might be'?" Diego pulled away his right hand and presented the reader with his open left palm.

She took the hand and stroked the warm skin. "The Life line is...Is slightly different from the last time. Here!"

She scraped her nail over the mid portion of his palm, where the line came to an abrupt end. "It's a star. A star at the end of the Life line. It... It wasn't there before."

"Meaning?"

"The star predicts a sudden upset in life, young man. But on your left palm...

'What might be'...But here. This line, this branch downward from the Life line...It's a dubious sign. And the Plain of Mars – the lines around it are poor, broken now."

"And the broken lines around Mars?" Baldock spoke with his hands clasped together.

The waitress stole a quick glance at Baldock then turned back to her friend. "Broken lines around the Plain of Mars, James. It means poor health...A short life." She grabbed the note that had been placed on the table and retreated to the coffee counter. "I...I'll be back with your change, sir."

"Keep the change!" Baldock called out from over his shoulder as he rose and threw on his overcoat. "It's for the entertainment."

"Thanks, Abby." Crantz jumped to his feet and fell in step behind the doctor. "I...I'll see you when I get back."

The waitress called out to her friend as he followed Baldock out the doorway. "Young man!"

Crantz turned around.

"Aye!...Ye're still a young man, James." The waitress squeezed her hands together. "I donna why but...I feel ye shouldn't go. The left palm, 'what might be'...It's no good, James. I feel it's no good."

Diego smiled. "Thanks, Abby. Don't worry about me. I am doing what I've always wanted to do." He waved. "I'll see you when I get back." He turned and let the door close softly behind him.

Chapter Nine
Five Days Later

Diego Crantz sat at the desk, the small lamp barely enough to light the page that he had inked with William Jude Gregor's verse. The tiny flat had filled with the aroma of the meal he had readied for six p.m. He looked at his watch then stared at the words he had written: 'Death and sweet life, one sorrow, one bliss...Each one denied...'

Probably meaningless poesie by a man yearning for something...Something. The botanist creased the paper, stretched each fold with a kitchen knife then flew the airplane across the hallway, landing his aircraft in the blackness of the closet. He stood up and walked back to the kitchen.

Marian Priest shook her tired head and tried the second key on the deadbolt. Three keys for the door and they all looked the same. The dabs of red and green paint, meant to tell them apart, had worn off weeks ago...Almost four years now and still she never seemed to choose the right key – especially when she was tired. And she was always tired.

The resident doctor wasn't looking forwards to another night alone. She could have stayed at work longer.

At least she would have had company in the hospital but the sound of the old folks—the geriatrics – confused old souls, always seemed worse at night. There was only so much a person could take, even if that person was training to be a geriatrician.

She pushed open the door to her apartment and peeled off her raincoat. The drips of cold spring water curled across her sleeve and fell to the rubber mat. Marian sniffed the air. A waxy smoke...A candle. She hadn't left a candle burning and even if she had, it wouldn't be burning twelve hours later. What-?

"Surprise!" The hall lights lit up and a tall figure, party hat in place and wine glass in hand, filled the doorway to the kitchen. "You promised that while I was away you would be in bed by seven every night, Marian." Diego looked at his watch. "You're an hour late and...Dinner is waiting."

"And you promised that you would call me as soon as you got back. When did you get in?" Marian didn't wait for an answer. She leaned into her husband's chest and pulled his body close. "Do you have any idea how hard it is to come home to an empty apartment, Diggy? To a dark hallway? Macaroni dinner?"

She kissed him hard on the lips. "I'm sure glad you can cook." She smiled. "But the worst part was the lonely nights…Dinner first!..Five days of hell, Mr. Crantz. Don't do it again!"

Diego pulled her to him and slipped his hand along the smooth skin of her lower back.

"Later! I need to eat!"

"Guess what?" Diego smiled. "It'll be Dr. Crantz, Ph.D, Chief of Botanical Research – New Age Pharma!"

Diego switched on the light over the dinner table and presented his wife with a document. "Dr. Baldock showed me around his lab – it covers over two city blocks just outside Seattle. That took almost three days. He wanted me to see everything! Everything! Every little facet of his operation. I met people I had only ever read about in pharmacology journals, research papers!"

His face flushed a deep crimson. "Baldock has put together a world class group. In the last few weeks, he's brought in three men from independent drug firms to sit on his board—just for this one project! There's, there's..." His hands twisted excitedly. "There's Dr. Kardon of Bridge Genomics, Dr. Ralph Hutcheons...His firm is really big! 'Future's Pharmakinetics'. Everybody's heard about F.P. And then there is Dr. Gerry Goldberg. Goldberg's the most innovative mind in the whole pharmaceutical industry, Marian!"

Diego reached over and pulled the lid off the serving tray that sat in the middle of the table. "Duck a l'orange!"

He motioned for his wife to sit. "It's a little over done but that's because you promised me you would be home by six." He filled her glass with wine and raised a toast. "To the girl I missed and will always love."

"To the man I've always loved and always miss." Marian pulled her thick, black hair off the back of her neck. "Let me wash up but keep on talking. Tell me what he said. Is it full time? Is it what you wanted?"

"It's everything I wanted and...And it's more!" Diego watched his wife disappear around the corner and raised his voice above the sound of running water.

"After Baldock showed me the production facility, we drove across town to a second site. A small concrete shell in the suburbs – no name, not even an address on the building. But inside! Jesus! It was unbelievable! There were twenty technicians with the latest analytical instruments and machines. It's his new research arm—completely separate from his main business...For now. And it's all being geared up for one new drug...One seed." The botanist fell silent for a moment. "And then, we talked."

Marian returned to the table and threw her arms around her husband again. "About a job?"

"It's more than a job. I'll be running the botanical research facility – New Age Pharma's innovative laboratory, its new research arm. It's a chance to change the world with its very first product." He smiled. "And it's just across town from that job you were offered in the Veteran's Hospital – the position you said you would take."

Marian beamed. "When? When does it start? You know I'm done here in three months. They want me to start at the 'Vets' July 1st. We could move back together! Did Dr. Baldock say when he wanted you to begin?"

"As soon as we get back from South America." He squeezed her hand. "One more trip – a few weeks this time, I'm afraid."

Marian sighed. "Macaroni and lonely nights." She stared at her husband with dark brown eyes. "How long?"

"Five weeks – eight at the most. It's a mountain climb, high altitude. We have to acclimatize on the way up." Diego nodded. "My Uncle Karl will be with us. He knows the area."

"Why? What are you looking for on top of a mountain?"

"One plant...One very special plant." Crantz grinned. "It's the one that I helped Baldock find at Kew...It's the one that will change the world."

Diego stood up and served a slice of steaming duck. "It's a unique plant...Very unusual. Baldock has invested a lot of money in this project. He...He really believes that he's on to one of the world's great discoveries."

"The world's next wonder drug?" Marian shook her head. "In medicine, new discoveries are more often like the stock market–great hype followed by a lot of disappointment. It's the treatments – the ones that evolve, evolve slowly through hard work and steady research— which usually become the real wonder drugs."

The botanist nodded. " Dr. Baldock hasn't achieved his success through stabs in the dark or lucky bets, Marian. We talked about the product...What we hope will be the final product. And it will probably be years before the drug reaches the market." He smiled. "That's why my contract with New Age is long term."

"So, what is the product?" Her eyes smiled. "A new antibiotic, heart drug? Or is it the latest sleepy time herbal tea?"

"I suppose I could grind it up and make it into a tea!" He smiled and shrugged his shoulders. "But if it is all that he says it is, you might be put out of business."

"I'm a geriatrician. I take care of old people, Diggy. Nature has an unstoppable supply of patients for my specialty!" She stared at her husband for a moment. "So what is it!?"

"Dr. Baldock claims that the plant – the seed of the plant – has the capacity to significantly extend the normal human lifespan."

"A longevity drug. Maybe...An immortality drug." Diego frowned. "I've seen some of the preliminary data, the actual living cells! Work by one of his colleagues! Cells from the man's own hand – grown in a test tube!"

He sighed. "The volume of seed has been very limited to date. And the studies... Most of the studies have been uncontrolled. Not really scientific."

"What do you mean, not scientific?"

"The man tried it on himself! Not Baldock! I mean his colleague, the one who found the plant." He shook his head. "The man ingested the seed then took samples of his own skin tissue, the inside lining of his stomach, even three biopsies of his liver and put them under a microscope. And each specimen...Each specimen taken one week apart, showed cellular rejuvenation. Over a period of weeks, the man's cells became younger!"

"What about chemistry?" Marian nodded. "Microscopic appearances can be deceiving sometimes. Did he perform analyses on the cell contents, the DNA?"

Diego nodded. "Some tests but...Nothing that was complete, by any means. The reports suggested changes in the cellular contents of free radicals – the breakdown products of normal cell function. And something called telo...Telom-"

"Telomeres."

"That's it. The tail ends of the chromosomes – the genetic strings in each cell." The botanist wiped his lips. "In normal aging, the tails on the ends of each chromosome – the telomere – shortens as the cell divides. Once the cell divides a certain number of times, the telomere gets to a certain length and the cell dies. Sort of a programmed death sentence from the day that cell is created." Diego shook his head. "Each one of our cells... Each one of us is destined to die the moment we are born."

Silence filled the small dining room. Then Marian said, "Everyone thinks they want to live forever...But there's always been one problem."

"What's that?"

"Modern science can keep people alive beyond their normal years but the situation isn't always what the patient wants."

"Death may be better?" Diego frowned.

"It's like the ancient Greek myth – the story of Tithonus." The doctor placed her knife and fork carefully onto the edge of her plate.

"He was a Trojan prince who became the lover of Eos, the goddess of dawn. They were so much in love that Eos asked Zeus to grant Tithonus eternal life but...She forgot to ask Zeus to grant her lover eternal youth as well. Tithonus lived forever but his body withered and Eos locked him away."

"Immortality and youth." A weak smile creased her lips. "Tell your new boss that the two have to go hand in hand. Otherwise...The goddess will lock him away."

Marian looked down at her fingers and squeezed them together. "And with any new drug, there are always wrong turns, blind alleys...New discoveries that aren't always what they appear to be. A thousand pitfalls, things that turn bad."

"Baldock knows what he's doing...I know what I'm doing, Marian."

She nodded and looked up. "I know you do, Diggy...I'm sure that Dr. Baldock does, too."

"After all, he did hire you as head of research...I just don't want...It's just that I miss you already."

Marian sighed. "You know I'm a worrier. I...I want you to...I don't want you to be the hero of the world, Diggy...I just want you to be mine."

Diego smiled. "I can do that...I can be your hero." He leaned across the table and caressed her cheek. "Don't worry. I'll be back soon and tomorrow...Tomorrow will be here before you know it."

Chapter Ten
Veteran's Administration Hospital, Seattle
Two and a Half Years Later

"This eighty-six year old lady broke her right hip five days ago." Marian Priest glanced down at the chart then nodded at one of the medical students. "Jonathan. Tell me what is particular about this case. Why did this lady break her hip?"

The student reddened then shrugged his shoulders. "She...She must have taken a fall – tripped, lost her balance."

"Sure." Marian nodded. "Imbalance in the elderly. That can be a factor." She looked down at her chart again. "But Mrs. Olafson's injury wasn't a fall. Was it Mrs. Olafson?"

The old lady's lips parted into a toothless grin. She bent forwards on her dowager's hump and exclaimed, "Heavens no, dear! I just had this sudden pain right here." She rubbed the outside of her thigh. "And then I fell to the ground. Oh no! It's because-"

"Mrs. Olafson." The doctor placed a gentle hand onto her patient's shoulder and held her forefinger up to her lips.

The patient let out a girlish giggle. "I...I forgot, doctor."

"The patient didn't trip. And she didn't fall." Marian Priest looked at the three students, their wide eyes alert, anxious to learn. She sighed then smiled at her patient.

Mrs. Olafson had already finished dinner by the time the doctor and her charges had arrived in her room – the last patient on teaching rounds. The geriatrician paused. Just tell them, she thought but...No. Facts can be learned from a book but teaching... Teaching is the art of showing your students how to think. "A lot of older people fall and don't become patients. So...So why Mrs. Olafson? Always listen to the patient. Did you all hear what she said?"

Priest shook her head. "The patient did not fall. She had a pain here." The doctor tapped her own thigh. "Then...After the pain had started, she fell to the ground."

"Linda." Marian pointed to a petit girl. She had to be at least in her early twenties to be in third year medical school but her small face and her fine hands made her look like a high school student.

"Olafson...That's a Scandinavian name." The student nodded and her eyes narrowed. "My grandmother broke both her hips...She was from Norway. I remember that she had once told me that soft bones was a family problem, that-"

"Right! Genetic background! Who you are! Where you're from!" Priest squeezed her patient's arm. "And Mrs. Olafson is a grandmother too!"

The old lady smiled.

"Osteoporosis!" The last student blurted out the words. "The brittle bone broke and then the patient fell!"

"Bull's eye, Jeff!" Marian's lips parted into a triumphant grin. "And what else tells you that this lady has osteoporosis?"

"Female, elderly, post-menopausal. "He started to smile.

"Good." Priest nodded. "And look at Mrs. Olafson's back."

The patient smiled. "I am your storybook little old lady...But I used to be taller."

Jonathan answered. "Osteoporotic compression fractures. Brittle bones of the spine collapse and the patient actually loses height."

"That's right. Sometimes up to four inches in height. Now..." The doctor gently pulled the patient's hands out from under the bed sheets and placed a spoon into her right palm. "Look at Mrs. Olafson's hands.

The three students gathered around and watched as the patient tried to grip the metal handle, pretending to ladle soup from an invisible bowl. After four or five tries, her twisted fingers lost their hold and the spoon fell to the floor. She sighed. "It makes every day impossible without help from my daughter."

"Arthritis." Linda looked up. "Bad arthritis."

"What kind of arthritis, Linda?"

The student shook her head.

"Then what would you expect to be a treatment the patient might receive for this arthritis?"

The student's face lit up. She turned to the patient and asked, "Mrs. Olafson. What kind of medication do you take at home?"

The patient laughed. "I'm so glad it was you who asked, dear. Dr. Priest told me not to give you any hints – no hints at all, she said...I have rheumatoid arthritis and I take prednisone five milligrams twice a day."

"Very good!" Marian Priest closed the chart, thanked the patient then led her charges out of the room. "So, for any patient. Never forget to ask what drugs they've been taking...And osteoporosis? Predisposing factors?" She pointed at the first student.

"Elderly female – postmenopausal."

Priest pointed at Linda.

"Genetic background – caucasian, northern European ancestry."

"Two more factors that we saw here this evening."

"Her medication, her prednisone." Jeff twisted his hands. "And...Ahhhhh-"

"Rheumatoid arthritis." Priest nodded. "It's a disease that compounds this patient's brittle bone problem...As if she needs anything else to deal with! All these factors make Mrs. Olafson a time bomb just waiting to break. She-"

The squeal of her pager cut short the doctor's words. "Okay. That's it for tonight. I'll see you three back here at 8:00 a.m." Marian smiled at her students then clipped her pager off her belt and scanned its messages. '5216' – it was a local she didn't recognize, a ward that had never called her before.

The geriatrician walked over to the nursing station and dialed the number.

"Memorial Ward. Palliative Care."

"It's Dr. Priest. You must have paged me by mistake."

"Oh, Dr. Priest! Thank you for answering so quickly. You...You took care of my father when he was in VA last month with his heart – George Madison? "The nurse's voice faltered. "You did so much for him...Thank you. But I was calling you about a patient here on Memorial Ward who has requested you as his doctor. He-"

"I'm sorry. I only work in VA proper." Marian stifled a yawn. "I don't see patients on the private ward."

"Yes. I understand." The nurse cleared her throat. "I am the nurse administrator here at Memorial. This patient is a man who says he knows you. I mean...Knows your husband."

"My husband is...Dead."

There was a moment of silence then the nurse continued. "I'm...I'm sorry. I hadn't realized that Mr. Priest had passed away." There was a pause. "This is very strange, doctor...I...I admitted the patient myself—diagnosis is 'end-stage adenocarcinoma of the lung'...But he was very insistent. He said that he had to have you as his doctor and...He definitely said that he knows your husband."

Silence again.

"Dr. Priest?"

"Yes."

"The admission itself is very unusual. It's completely funded by a third party. The man has no insurance...But the company that's paying the bill is reputable and has posted a bond far beyond what we would normally charge. It's a well known drug firm here in Seattle—'New Age Pharma'."

Marian felt a searing burn in the pit of her stomach and clutched at the top of the counter.

"It says in the chart that the patient knows your husband, Dr. Diego…No last name…I didn't know that your husband was a doctor."

Marian swallowed hard. "A botanist…My husband was a botanist but he never finished his Ph.D. He…He disappeared on a trip to South America and…"

"Dr. Priest? The patient is quite insistent that you be his physician and…" The nurse sighed. "When we talked this afternoon, he told me that he knows your husband. Knows him…In the present tense, I mean. And that…"

"That what?"

"I don't want to meddle in personal affairs. He said that he wants to tell you himself, tell you…"

"Tell me what?! Is this some sort of twisted-?!"

"Oh no! This patient is dying. Dying people are very sincere." The nurse paused. "Please don't say that I told you but I believe that the best thing for the dying is that they are given what they need…And this patient truly needs you, Dr. Priest."

"Tell me what then?"

The nurse sighed. "The patient talks about your husband as though he were very much alive and that…That he has a message from him."

Marian felt a cold chill, hopeful and desperate, surge up her spine. "What's the patient's name?"

There was a flutter of papers. "The man's name is Crantz…Mr. Karl Crantz."

Chapter Eleven

She watched the patient from the doorway, a frail body each breath barely able to lift the white sheets that clung to his emaciated chest. Dying rays of pink sunset penetrated the dark room then danced on the whitewash of the ceiling, turned by the slats of the window blinds. Marian touched the sign on the half-closed doorway – 'DO NOT DISTURB'.

"He said that when you come, to ignore the sign." The nurse nodded to the doctor.

The man's profile – the curve of his nose, his chin— the way he rested his head on the pillow...It all seemed so familiar, so much like Diggy but so much more frail, sickly, older.

Marian shook her head and stepped back, away from the doorway. "No...I...I can't."

"You can't?"

"No...I can't be his doctor. It would be unprofessional. He's family...Too much history. Too...Too many questions." She handed the chart back to the nurse. "Tell him...Tell him I'm sorry. I'll get Dr. MacDermott to take him on and I'll come to visit...To talk but-"

"But Mr. Crantz said that if you don't take him on as a patient, he'll leave, check himself out!" The nurse's eyes widened. "And the man can't take care of himself. He has nowhere to go! He-"

"No!" Marian clenched her jaw tight. "You don't understand. Just tell him-"

"Dr. Priest?...Is that you, Dr. Priest?" A faint voice, hoarse and weak echoed from the room.

The doctor shuddered and drew her clammy hand across her forehead then rested it on the back of her neck. The coolness of her palm soothed the taut muscles and her shoulders relaxed. "Tell him that I need to think." She turned and escaped down the hallway.

The drive home took less than fifteen minutes but to Marian it seemed like hours. The image of the man haunted her thoughts – face like parchment, eyes sunk deep into their sockets, a man whose life could not change course, a feeble body, a dying soul.

This patient was like so many others she had already treated in her short career but this one...Diggy's uncle...She could see her husband so clearly...So clearly in the silhouette of his tortured face.

She parked the car on the street and quietly unlocked the door of her modest townhome. They were asleep again...Before she could make it home.

Marian picked up the two toy trucks that had been made to crash in front of the fireplace then knelt next to the couch where the child and woman lay cuddled together.

Marian kissed the boy and grandma then tucked the cover over the two warm bodies. She climbed the stairs and collapsed into bed. She fell asleep knowing that morning would come too soon and she had so much to think about, so much to ask the man who wanted to be her patient.

"It's here, Marian! Just a little higher!" Diego's eyes glistened and his blond hair swirled in the never ending gust of wind. "Come on!"

She could see him – tall, handsome. He was standing next to Uncle Karl – the same height, the same build but older, so much older than Diggy.

Diego motioned for her to follow then the two men started up the mountain.

Marian shook her head and placed her hand on the back of her neck but the knot in her muscles wouldn't ease, her shoulders stayed tight. The wind whipped her hair – each gust stronger, growing stronger.

Soon, she could barely see them – the two men just miniatures on the glistening slope, small specks of black pocked onto the white ice.

The squall continued its siege on the mountain. It whipped her dark hair across her eyes, transforming the scene before her from white…To gray…Then to darkness…All darkness.

The doctor tossed in her bed then finally awoke with the last image of her dream – the darkness - engraved on her consciousness. Her husband's voice echoed in her head. "Uncle Karl, old Uncle Karl…So much like Diggy…He can tell you…Karl has a message."

Chapter Twelve

Marian Priest tucked the patient's chart under her arm. She entered the room, closed the door silently then turned on the light at the bedside table.

The man let out a weak groan, his eyelids fluttered. Two opaque, holes opened and stared at the intruder. There was a flicker, a brief spark of recognition then the blue eyes darkened again. He smiled. "You are...Dr. Priest?"

The doctor pulled a chair over to the bedside and slowly sat down. "She nodded. "Uncle Karl...You are Uncle Karl?"

Karl Crantz smiled but did not reply. He gazed at her for a moment then said, "Come closer, please. My...My eyes are weak. They say I have cataracts."

There was a moment of silence then the patient spoke in a hushed tone. "You... You are even more beautiful than Diego could describe."

"You..." Marian wiped the moistness from her eyes. "Last year, the American consulate in La Paz told me that my husband was lost...Killed on the mountain. That you and he had died in an avalanche... Missing... Missing high in the mountains for nearly two years... Then they had found what was left. They-"

"No!" The man's voice was firm. "Diego said that he wouldn't let himself die... Not without..."

"Without what?"

Crantz grabbed at the edge of the bed sheet with gnarled fingers. Each bony wrist was twisted at an angle that prevented his digits from closing down firmly on their target. He winced, quickly tucked his hands beneath the sheets then pinned the cover between his stiff claws and pulled it over his chest. "Not without letting you know... Letting you know how much he loved you."

"Loved me? Is he?...What's the message that -?"

The patient held up a naked finger. "Diego said that I must tell you, I must...Must show you...Diego loved you, Marian. He loved you more than any words could describe but-"

"Then where is he?! Dammit! If he loved me so much why did he go? He knew it was dangerous! Why didn't he...Why didn't he come back home?" She buried her face in her hands.

Karl Crantz stared at the visitor. He closed his eyes and asked, "You will take me on as a patient...Won't you?"

The doctor did not respond.

"I...I won't be difficult." Crantz tilted his head at the walker that stood next to his bed. "I can still get around. I don't need babying, just...Just some help."

Marian nodded and gazed back at the emaciated figure. She took in a deep breath. "Whenever...Whenever I take on a new patient – a patient in your condition, Uncle Karl, I always make it clear what my role is. That-"

"That you cannot save me."

"That's right." She stood up and walked over to the window. "You have a terminal illness. Nothing...No one can keep you from dying...But I can make you as comfortable as possible."

Karl smiled. "Thank you, Dr...Dr. Priest. You are-"

"Call me Marian." She turned to face the patient, her arms crossed over her chest. "You're my patient but you're also my uncle...Diego's uncle."

"Then call me Karl...Uncle makes me feel old...Older than I really am." He turned and gazed at the window.

The doctor sat back down and leaned forwards on her chair. Angry tears filled her eyes. "What happened? Did he hurt? Why...Why couldn't he-?"

"The message is that...There came a point in time when he was not the same man you once knew." Karl's voice quivered. "Diego...He wanted to come back. He needed to come back but...But he could never be the same."

The doctor shook her head. "I don't know what you mean. I want to know why. I want to know what happened, how-"

"I will tell you what happened." Crantz stared at the doctor. "That is why I came. To tell you the story...To explain. Then you can understand...You can understand how much he really loved you. And...His love for you lives on."

"Diego is gone but his love isn't?"

The patient ignored the question. "It's a long story. If you have time, Marian...If God gives me that time...I will tell you." He looked up. "Please...A glass of water."

The doctor filled a cup from the ice pitcher and held it to the patient's lips.

Crantz smiled. "Thank you." His shaking hand, draped in the bed sheet, held tight to hers.

"I introduced Diego and Baldock to the Kallahuaya, the Andean healer—an old man I had met many years ago...A very special man. I met your husband and that...That bastard Baldock." He shivered. "I met them at the airstrip when they flew in...When they flew in to Chajaya."

Chapter Thirteen
Chajaya, Bolivia

The helicopter rattled as it jerked to a landing, half-choked on the thin air of the altiplano. Gideon Baldock was the first to step out of the aircraft, his gray-blond hair whipped by the wind of the chopper blades that slowly spun to a stop. Diego Crantz followed, his eyes drawn, his face pale. He had not had time to catch up with the jet lag – London to Buenos Aires then a run to catch the connection to La Paz.

Baldock had been waiting for him at the airport. Diego's new boss had arrived in the Bolivian capital ten days before and had already acclimatized to the twelve thousand foot elevation. And then the helicopter ride higher still to the northern mountains and the small town of Chajaya.

"Uncle Karl!" Diego's voice reverberated in the wide, empty space of the landing pad. The helicopter was the only functional aircraft sitting on the lonely runway surrounded by grassy fields and snow-capped peaks. An old Cessna crouched at the far end of the pot-holed airstrip, its left wing tipped into the dirt, its rudder bent and hanging on to the body by one rusted wire.

The tall man who approached the newcomers wore a Panama straw hat, brown from sweat and years of wear.

Beneath the hat, the earflaps of a multi-colored Andean skullcap twisted in the wind in rhythm with the wool poncho wrapped around his broad shoulders.

Karl Crantz closed his broad arms around his nephew. His blue eyes disappeared into his weathered face. "You still look the same, Diego! And now you're as tall as your uncle!...How's my boy?"

"Good! Tired but good!" Diego turned to Baldock. "Dr. Baldock, this is my Uncle Karl. You probably know each other quite well from your telephone conversations.

The two men shook hands then Diego returned to the aircraft to unload the bags.

"Don't bother to unload, Diego!" The mountaineer turned to Baldock. "Your things will be safe in the helicopter overnight, doctor. I've arranged for some pack animals at the base of the mountain but we'll have to fly to Chupiorco. The road washed out last week and I hear that two or three trucks went with the road. This time of year..." He shook his head. "It probably can't be repaired until the weather dries out."

"The herbalist? Did you find the man who knows about the plant?" Baldock's jaw jutted out at their host.

Crantz nodded. "The Kallahuaya...I have met ten or twelve of these medicine men over the years. When I mentioned that I wanted to show a western doctor a plant that could make a man young again, each one knew what I was talking about. But...Not one of them would tell me anything – except that I should ask no more questions."

"But you told me on the phone that-!"

"Until I asked Nestor Alvarez...Come!" The mountaineer opened the door to his jeep and climbed in. "That's who we will see in the morning, Dr. Baldock"

Karl Crantz turned the key in the ignition and the old Toyota growled to life. The vehicle bounced off the runway then pushed a path through the grassy fields heading for a cluster of lights that twinkled in the dying light of the day. "Nestor is the oldest of the Kallahuaya, paralyzed on his right side—dying, slowly dying. When I saw him, I wasn't sure that he would still be here when you arrived. But the old man insisted that he meet you. He said that he had to be sure that you were the right one, Dr. Baldock."

Baldock stared at the mountains. "The right one for what, Karl?"

The driver shrugged. "I can't be sure what he meant. Just that-"

"I'm tired." Baldock crossed his arms over his chest. "This quacky herbalist better have more to say than that." He scowled at Crantz. "He knows where it is? How to get there?"

Crantz nodded. "Nestor Alvarez knows the plant you want and the man is not a quack. He is a respected practitioner of an ancient art, a man who-"

"When do we meet him?"

"In the morning...Just after the dawn we will head up that mountain." Crantz pointed to the western peak. "Half-way to the top is where the man lives...If he is still alive."

"And if he isn't?"

"Then I can take you to the northern peak of Chupiorco but..." Crantz shook his head. "That was all Nestor would tell me...That what you want is at the northern peak."

Darkness had fallen swiftly and the night was bright with the shimmering of thousands of stars in a moonless sky. Karl Crantz parked the jeep at the corner of a small plaza and jumped out. "Chajaya. We have a pension here for the night, gentlemen." He glanced at Baldock's grim face. "Don't worry, doctor. Nestor is a man of his word and he told me that he had made a promise that he would not die."

"This mountain witch doctor wants to see me so bad, he can ward off death?" Baldock shook his head.

"It wasn't me he made the promise to." Crantz led his guests into a stone house. "Nestor said that he had made a promise to a man years ago, a man he had met on Chupiorco."

Crantz pulled off his hat and poncho then poured some water from a pitcher into a stone basin. A naked light bulb flickered from the ceiling of the small room. "Choose your places, gentlemen." He pointed to the two worn mattresses that sprawled beneath the light.

"Where are you going to sleep, Uncle Karl?" Diego yawned and pulled his hand over his drawn face.

"Mine is the stone corner." The older man smiled. "Just like the mountain, Diego."

"This herbalist says he met someone on the mountain?" Baldock had already stretched out on the thickest of the beds.

Karl reached to the ceiling and pulled the cord that extinguished the light. "The Kallahuaya have a special language. They use it mostly among themselves, when they talk about medicines. But when I saw him last, Nestor seemed confused. He spoke to me partly in Quechua but he used some words from his own language."

Crantz sighed. "My knowledge of either language is far from perfect."

There was a period of silence in the cold, dark room then Karl Crantz added, "Nestor called him the man of the mountain...No...No. That's not quite right. The Quechua words he used were...Nestor Alvarez told me that he promised he would not die before he had found the right man. That's it...Not before he had found the right man."

Crantz nodded to himself. "The old man said he had made that promise many years ago to the...Yes! That's the words he used! That's what Nestor called the man. Nestor made that promise to the 'Spaniard of the northern peak'."

Chapter Fourteen

The next morning began before the sun could paint the eastern sky. Thick mist had engulfed the town overnight and the trio left Chajaya in a wet darkness that muffled the sound of the old Toyota. They headed due west down to the base of the valley and reached the bottom just as the first light pierced the night.

Diego looked back and saw Chajaya surrounded by dark fields on the central slopes of the valley, small, wisps of smoke wearing away from within at the thinning dank cloak.

The jeep bounced and rolled on the rock-laden road as it passed from one side of the valley back again to the Chajaya side fording the stream that cut the valley in two. At the first crossing, the water flooded the sides of the old vehicle.

But with each pass across the waterway, each time heading higher, the water spread wider, shallower until, at their last crossing, the tires rolled over cobbles of stepping stones, turning faster slipping off at each fourth or fifth stone, spitting up wet rock and twisted clumps of mud.

After more than three hours, Karl pulled his vehicle over next to a large boulder and stopped.

He signaled for his guests to follow. The trio stumbled along a rocky road that headed straight up the hillside. The trail became narrower as it rounded a corner, less than a shoulder width separating the stone bluff on the right side from the precipice that dropped off a hundred feet to the left.

At the end of the path, Karl pushed up a small incline then stopped. He stood with his hands on his hips and waited for his friends to catch up. "There. Just where the sunlight is starting to shine." He pointed with a scrawny finger. "Can you see them, Diego?"

Diego squinted at the shadows of boulders and rock. Two shapes moved about at the bottom of a scree – an old landslide, caked in patches with lichen and weeds. "Llamas. I see two of them."

"And behind the animals. Can you see the hut?"

In the oblique light of the morning, the rubble of the hillside blended in with the feeble trees that pocked the landscape. Diego shook his head.

"When we get closer then. But I am sure that they have already seen us." Karl headed off towards the llamas.

The three men were less than fifty yards from the animals before Diego realized that the hut his uncle had referred to was a stone box, built with the squared off pieces of broken rock. Each gray slab had been carefully placed and mortared forming a perfect square, ten paces wide and ten paces deep. The building backed up against the mountainside, gray rock continuous with gray rock.

Karl held up his hand and said, "We wait."

The mortar on the eastern side of the building – the side that led to the rubbled trail where the visitors now stood – had crumbled at the edge, leaving a six inch hole through which a tin pipe had been shoved. Wispy smoke drifted slowly out the pipe stunted by the chill of the morning air.

The quiet was disturbed by a boot that scraped against ground behind them.

Karl turned and nodded at the man who seemed to appear out of the rock. He spoke a few words in Quechua then he turned to Diego and Baldock. "This is Florentino. He is the adopted son of Nestor Alvarez."

A few more words were exchanged then Florentino walked past and led them towards the hut. The man's tattered poncho clung to his thin frame. His sunken cheeks were sallow and cold.

Karl spoke in a low tone. "Florentino has been taking care of the old man for almost a year now. Nestor had another stroke last week. He's been blind since then and has grown much weaker...Very weak. Any day could be his last."

They stooped though the doorway and entered the cold dark cabin.

It was a few moments before their eyes had adjusted to the dim light from the single candle that smoldered in the corner of the stone cavern. The flame shimmered and cast ghostly shadows across the barren walls.

In the far corner, away from the light, a small wooden shrine framed a human skull, its right eye socket narrowed by a shattered orbit. The skull lay perched on a bed of dried grass. A tin pot filled with fresh flowers sat on the stone floor at the shrine's edge. The hilt of an old Spanish sword, its blade lost to wear and rust, lay off to the side—a holy cross standing guard at a place of worship.

Between the candle and the shrine, a lone body wrapped in a poncho lay on its side perched on a stone platform. The man's breathing was labored, each gasp wheezing through plugs of mucous that seeped from his drooping lips. His eyes were fixed on the doorway, a cold, unblinking stare. As the three men approached his bed, he began to speak Spanish in a choked, guttural voice.

"Pachamama is Holy Earth from which we are born and where we return. She gives us food and medicine. She has power...Power like God..."

The old man sputtered and a stream of phlegm fell to the floor. "She has power like God. Some years she produces...Some years, she does not. But always, Pachamama makes us what we are...Because we become what we eat...We eat what we become."

Then he spoke in Quechua and motioned with his left arm.

Florentino called out from the doorway in broken English. "My father wishes to know which man is the one."

Karl turned and spoke a few words to the stepson.

Florentino answered, "Then my father will examine both of them. He will determine which man will carry the seed."

Baldock cursed and turned to Karl. "This was not meant to be a contest! I'm here for information."

Crantz cast a quick glance at Baldock and the doctor fell silent. He gave Diego a nudge and the younger man approached Alvarez.

The healer tugged on Diego's coat and pulled him down to the level of the stone bed. He shifted his body to the edge of the platform, dragging his limp right arm and leg. His hollow eyes stared into Diego's.

A cold, shaking hand stroked the young man's face. Probing fingers circled his eyes, the tips of the fingers brushed his cheeks then the old man grasped his hand with thumb and forefinger.

The botanist could feel the pressure of the old man's grip – light but firm, the healer's finger riding the wave of the pulse at his wrist.

After a moment, Alvarez shook his head and beckoned his son to the bedside.

Florentino stood up. "My father reads the voice of the wind and the silence of the rocks." He looked down at Diego. "This man cannot be the one...You." He motioned for Baldock to take Diego's place.

The doctor cursed, shook his head and muttered as he walked past Karl. "I'll play this man's stupid little game but with the money I'm paying you..."

Baldock crouched next to the dying man.

The Kallahuaya repeated the ceremony – fingers across the forehead, around the outline of the doctor's eyes. His touch stopped at the tip of Baldock's chin and the old man let out a silent gasp.

Alvarez's body began to shake. His blind eyes widened and his left hand clutched at Baldock's arm then slid down to his subject's wrist. The old man's head nodded. He closed his eyes and his parched lips began to mouth voiceless words.

Gideon Baldock and Nestor Alvarez stayed close for minutes but for the doctor it felt like hours. Finally, Baldock wrested his arm away from the dying man and stood up.

"Karl! I've indulged this old man long enough! Ask him! Ask him if he is going to tell me how to-"

"Yes." Florentino answered before Baldock could finish. "You are the one my father has been waiting for. You are the one who he promised to find."

"Then let's-"

Karl Crantz was already at Nestor's side. The healer clutched the mountaineer by the arm and began to talk quickly, quietly. After nearly thirty minutes of whispered words, Crantz nodded and stood up.

The patient clutched the bed sheets and grimaced. "I followed him – Florentino, I mean. After the talk with Nestor, Florentino told us we had to go – right away...That we had to leave right away."

"He was concerned about his step-father?"

"No. He was concerned...But not about Nestor." Crantz shook his head. "It was as if he had to be somewhere else, talk with someone else."

"Florentino sounds like a very strange man."

Karl nodded. "He started up the mountain. So I followed him...Not so as he could see me...At a distance."

Marian gazed at her patient, a puzzled look on her face. "Was this something unexpected from the Kallahuaya?...The sudden departure, wandering off? Was-"

"No, no! Florentino wasn't wandering. He was going somewhere...Somewhere special." Karl turned away.

"But Baldock and Diego were busy...Talking about different aspects of the climb, so I-"

"But you're the mountaineer, Karl. You're the expert. Why would the two of them talk about the climb if-"

"About the plant, I mean." Crantz gripped his hands together. "Baldock and Diego had to discuss different aspects of how they were to harvest specimens." He nodded. "That's it...So I decided to follow Florentino."

Silence.

"And where did you follow him to?"

"It wasn't far. About a half-hour climb from the hut. I thought I had lost him but then I heard some rocks slide – slowly, as if someone were moving them."

He watched the Kallahuaya from the end of the small rocky alcove, hidden in the shadow of a large boulder.

Florentino had finished placing the last of the stones to the side just as the sun crested the ridge. Its feeble morning rays filled the small doorway he had created with warming light. The Kallahuaya disappeared through the hole and dropped to his knees in front of an altar made of twigs and stones.

An ancient Spanish helmet sat on one corner of the hearth-shaped podium staring across at the empty eyes of a human skull. Between the two, a line had been drawn with pebbles – each one round and smooth, worn by water, wind and by eons of human touch.

Florentino picked away slowly, deliberately at the small stones, muttering words, a chant, his head bowed, his eyes on his work. With the last pebble gone, he quietly pushed the helmet and the skull closer...Slowly closer, until they touched.

He looked up and as he did, the sunlight pierced the small room and lit the ghostly skeleton of an old tree that stood in the shadow behind the altar. Leafless, lifeless, the plant rested, dried and cracked, leaning against the cold wall of the dark cave.

"Karl! Karl! Are you all right?" Marian Priest had one hand on her patient's wrist, the other massaging his neck, just beneath his chin.

"You blanked out for a moment...Your pulse slowed. Your heartbeat has changed...Very irregular. We'll have to do some tests."

She leaned over her patient. "Can you hear me?"

"It was like that! Just like that!" Crantz clutched his fist to his chest and stared straight ahead. "My heart wanted to pop right out of my chest when he saw me!"

"Karl! Can you hear me?" Marian shook his shoulder.

Crantz closed his eyes and took a deep breath. "Like an angel's voice, Marian...Like an angel's voice."

The doctor sat back down in the chair and pursed her lips. "There is something important you and I have to talk about before we go any further."

He smiled again. "I trust you. You're my doctor."

"It's not as doctor and patient that we have to talk. Not about this one thing, at least. It's about..." Marian stood up. "You know that I am your only next of kin, don't you?"

Crantz stared at the doctor.

"It's been nearly three years since Diego disappeared – hard on everyone." She turned away from the patient. "Just after Diego left, his mother was diagnosed with cancer of the pancreas and she died...Very quickly. Diego's father..."

Marian sat back down and buried her face in her arms. "He had lost his only son and then his wife...He said that he couldn't...He died in a car crash.....On Interstate 5."

Karl Crantz continued to stare.

"So, it's up to me...And you, Karl, to decide what we do...If your heart stops. How much effort do we put into resuscitation? How heroic should we be?"

A long silence followed then Crantz asked, "What would you want...What would you want if...If I were Diego?"

Marian shook her head and stood up. "If you were my husband, I would not be your treating physician. A treating physician has to stay emotionally detached. And if...If it were Diego in this bed...I wouldn't be able to do that."

She turned to face her patient. "But if you were my husband, with everything that I know about your medical condition..." She pointed at the binder that lay on the bed. "I would want a 'DO NOT RESUSCITATE' order on your chart." She nodded. "The suffering would end if tragedy hit."

Crantz nodded. "Then it's 'DO NOT RESUSCITATE'." He closed his eyes. "Thank you, doctor...Thank you, Marian."

Chapter Fifteen
The Next Day

"I had thought you weren't coming back." The patient pushed a note pad under the covers then clutched the sheets between his wrists. "That you had decided we were too close...You being my only kin, I mean."

Marian Priest shook her head and sat down at the bedside. "I have an overload of patients, Karl." She glanced at her watch. "I thought that I would make it home for supper but...I'll grab a sandwich from the fridge."

"Is this a doctor-patient visit?...Or are you here as my only relative, my next of kin?"

"Both." The doctor flipped open the chart. "They did the tests this morning."

Crantz nodded. "They poked and prodded. Left the tapes on my skin." He pulled the sheets off his chest and showed his doctor the contact tapes from the electrocardiogram.

"Episodes of bradycardia, no ischemic changes...Your electrolytes are normal but borderline." She continued to turn the pages. "Potassium down from your admission. I think that..." She looked up.

Karl smiled but said nothing.

"I'm sorry." Marian closed the chart. "That was the doctor part of the visit. Everything's fine. Pain control good?"

"My back was sore...Until you arrived." Crantz wheezed a deep breath followed by a wet cough. "Seeing you...Seems to make everything better."

The doctor stood up. "Show me. Is it here?" She reached over and gently palpated his lower back.

"Just...Just over to the right." He winced. "On that blade at the back. What's it called? The-"

"Iliac crest." Marian rubbed the brim of the pelvis where it pushed out from the patient's emaciated frame. "The bone scan that was done this morning was hot in that area."

"Meaning?"

"Meaning inflammatory reaction–probable metastatic disease. It's..." The doctor sat back down. "It's not unexpected. Your lung cancer has spread to the bones. In your pelvis, where it's sore—but there are also spots in your right hip, your spine and your left shoulder."

Crantz closed his eyes.

Marian repeated the question. "Pain control good?"

"Fine. It's just fine. I...I don't like how my head feels when I take that liquid, that pain killer. It's-"

"It's a narcotic. It can upset your stomach sometimes, make you feel light-headed. If the bone ache becomes intolerable..." She put her hand on her own pelvis. "Especially here. If the narcotic doesn't work then we can use radiation therapy to ease the pain. But you have to let me know how you're doing. Remember, Karl, my job is to make you feel comfortable."

Crantz was silent for a moment then he said, "Marian, can you remember how you and Diego met? I...I don't mean to pry-"

The doctor smiled and looked down at the floor. "I'll never forget how we met." She looked at her patient. "Did he tell you? You spent some time together. I'm sure you talked."

Crantz nodded. "He told me some things. He smiled just like you when he talked about it. I...I can't remember-"

"It was our last year of high school...Last month, I think!" Marian stood up and stared out the window at a grove of ornamental cherry trees, their pink petals in full bloom. "It was in one of the last labs for biology and we had to dissect a fetal pig." She spaced her fingers inches apart. "A poor little creature, pickled in formaldehyde – one pickle for each pair of students."

She laughed. "I had seen him in class – the cute guy at the back. And he would always have his eye on me – whenever I looked up, I'd catch him." She shook her head. "But he was so shy...And so was I."

"Then how-?"

"I was so studious, so punctual!" The doctor turned around. "I went out to a dance once with a couple of girl friends and my mother told me that if I came home on time, she would never let me use her car again!" She sighed. "And that biology lab was the first time I was ever late!"

Marian sat down next to the bed and turned the shade to cut the glare of the bedside light. "It was strange. I remember the dread I felt when I opened the door...The room was silent. Twenty-one students ready to cut into a dead pig!"

"And you sat down with Diego?"

"Diego saved me from the jaws of Ralph Youngward – 'the evil professor', we called him! As soon as he saw the door handle turn, Diego tipped his jar and the pickling juice flew across the table right onto Youngward's back."

She laughed. "The guy didn't even stop to throw chalk! That's what he usually did when he was upset. But he was going out on a hot date right after school and had on his best suit. The man flew out of his chair, ripped off his lab coat and ran to the scrub sink in the next room."

"And then?"

"As soon as I walked in, Diego pulled me to his side and we scooted off to the far corner of the lab! By the time Youngward came back, there was nobody at that table and just one open jar that looked like it had fallen off the shelf!"

Crantz smiled. "Is that when you called him-?"

"Diggy!" Marian laughed. "I...I was so nervous. I thought that Youngward would catch on! My stomach was in knots and I could hardly breathe! And when I went to thank him, I called him-"

"Diggy...He said that you called him Diggy."

She nodded. "For the life of me, I couldn't remember his name! I knew that it began with a 'D' but..." She shook her head.

"And that's what you always called him – Diggy?"

"When we were alone." Marian smiled. "He was always Diggy to me."

The room remained silent for a long while.

Marian sighed. "Diggy was always protecting me – trying to keep bad things at bay, trying to keep me from hurt...I had a cat once. I had found her on the highway – a small thing."

"She must have wandered from her home then become lost in the woods, infested with tics. Diggy and I cleaned her, cared for her and then, one day, she just disappeared."

"And then?"

"Three years later the neighbor told me that the cat had been hit by a car." She squeezed her eyes shut. "Diggy had found her, buried her but...He couldn't bring himself to tell me that she had died."

Marian sighed. "He always tried to keep me from the hurt. Diggy was always my hero." Her voice faltered and she turned her gaze away from the patient. "My hero…"

Karl shut his eyes then stared out the window. "There are not many people... Who can feel each other so well. Who can-"

"He was very brave."

Crantz pulled back a breath. "Dig-, I mean Diego?"

"I never told him...It was one of the things that I admired so much in him – his fear."

"But you said that he was brave?"

Marian nodded. "A person can only be brave when he's afraid—otherwise there's nothing to be brave about. And Diego was afraid of so many things—things he wouldn't tell me about."

She stared out the window again. "He used to hate dissecting animals – worms, frogs, fetal pigs. It made him cringe. I could see it in his eyes but...But I could also see his courage."

"Diego...My Diggy was afraid to dissect animals…He was especially afraid to meet girls and, I can't imagine how we would ever have met if he hadn't acted on that urge."

She chuckled. "The urge to pour pickling juice onto the teacher!...Just at the right time, I guess."

The patient shifted his legs under the sheets and winced.

"You don't look very comfortable."

Crantz nodded. "I'm okay...I'm comfortable... Comfortable when you're here, Marian. Last night...When you came into the room. It was the first time I had felt comfortable since we left the stone hut where Nestor Alvarez died."

"The healer? He died?"

The patient nodded. "We left Chajaya the next morning. The word reached us just as we boarded the helicopter."

Crantz stared out the window. "The three of us had loaded the aircraft with supplies and had just strapped ourselves in. For some reason, the engine wouldn't turn."

"Baldock said that the blades...The blades of the chopper couldn't grip the thin air and that was why there was more strain on the motors but..."

"Florentino, Nestor's step-son – he's a very strange man." Karl furrowed his brow. "Baldock's temper was beginning to run thin and the man was slamming his fists onto the control panel, cursing, trying again and again to get the engine to catch and then the motor died altogether...Silence. No sputter, no whining blades. And, at that precise moment...At that precise moment!...Florentino appeared next to the helicopter...Out of nowhere!"

"That's not strange. You were distracted." Marian shrugged. "While you concentrated on the helicopter-"

"No." Crantz shook his head. "I...I had felt uncomfortable."

"I mean really uncomfortable since we had left the Kallahuaya. I had never felt that way before. Almost panicky and...And I was ready to jump. I had been looking all around while Baldock tried to start the engine. Where to run to. It was like something inside me was saying that I...I didn't belong in that helicopter and..."

"And everywhere I looked on that airstrip there was nothing, nothing for miles except the short grass twisting in the wind...Always the wind." He shook his head. "There was no one there."

Crantz took a deep breath then swallowed hard. "I can remember it so well, Marian! As if everything...Everything was in slow motion – just for that moment... Florentino was standing in the grass, his body moving...Moving with the wind...Like he was part...Just part of the field. Standing there—on my side of the helicopter."

He swallowed again and cleared a wad of phlegm from deep in his throat. "The wind – it was so...So rough. It whipped the field, the grass. But I remember the tassels...The tassels of his skullcap didn't move at all. The threads just hung there, straight, unmoving against his face – that face was…Was so thin, so cold."

The patient leaned up on his elbow and looked at the doctor. "You know...It was if the man was there on the airstrip, next to the helicopter but, at the same time...He wasn't." He fell back onto his pillow and shook his head. "It was the strangest thing."

"And in the silence, when...When the motor had died and the wind had suddenly stopped, Florentino looked directly at me...At me! And he spoke just three words, 'Nestor is dead'."

"Baldock laughed but I stared at the man and he stared back as if...As if he wanted to tell me...Tell ME something very important."

The patient turned to his doctor. "There's a special feeling. You know...When you leave a place but, deep down, you realize that someday you'll be back – that, when you're very much older, you'll be back."

Marian nodded.

"That was how I felt when I was staring at Florentino that day. I knew that I would be back to that place but that place was...Was Florentino."

"Did he say anything-?"

"Nothing else. Just 'Nestor is dead'." Crantz clutched the blanket. "Then the motor fired, the blades began to spin. I looked over at Baldock. His curses had turned to laughter. He...He was laughing for no reason except that the helicopter was about to take off. And when I looked back...Florentino was gone."

Marian pursed her lips. "Memories, Karl, can sometimes become twisted with time – especially when you're under stress. The man-"

"No!" The patient sat up in bed. "My body is dying, Marian but my mind is still all there!"

"Did...Did you talk to Diego about the man...About Florentino?" Marian looked down at her hands. "Sometimes Diggy...Sometimes Diego noticed things about people. Sometimes-"

"Diego didn't say anything but, in his eyes..." Karl swallowed hard. "In his eyes, I could see that he was afraid. He was-"

"He was brave." The doctor nodded. "He must have sensed something...Something." She looked up. "Did you ever go back to that place? Did you see Florentino again?"

Crantz nodded. "Yes I did – when I was very...Very much older." He let his body fall back onto the mattress. "But that day, we flew to Chupiorco."

Chapter Sixteen
The Helicopter to Chupiorco

"It's strange that he died. Just after he met you, I mean." Karl Crantz talked quietly into the microphone at his chin.

"You say it's strange, Uncle Karl?" Diego sat perched on a small box behind the pilot's seat. "The whole thing was strange, if you ask me! Nestor Alvarez, that little hole he lived in! And especially his son. What was his name?" He pushed the earpiece against his head, barely able to hear his uncle above the roar of the engines.

"Florentino. He was Nestor's stepson and a well-respected healer in his own right. A very intelligent-"

"Quack!" Baldock turned to Karl and sneered. "I've seen a lot of these types. Chinese herbalists, Hindu holy men, Indian shamans!" He shook his head. "Witches! Same sort of thing. Not that long ago, we used to burn them!"

The helicopter coughed, dipped then clutched the air and finally began to climb towards the north.

"The worst thing," Baldock continued, "is that sometimes these witch doctors find something that's useful – something that we can develop, something that would be worthwhile marketing. But..." He shook his head. "These guys are so into themselves, so into their superstitions, they have no real knowledge of the value, the usefulness of the product!"

"Like Gregor's seed?" Diego leaned forwards and poked his head between the two men seated in front.

"I believe that we'll find this plant is one of the best examples of what I'm talking about, Diego." Baldock nodded and adjusted his mouthpiece. "Nestor, that old bastard, has known about it for years. Years! And has he studied it? Has he used it? Has he told anybody who might be interested – somebody who could take the thing and change it into a useful product? Has he told anyone that there may be something up there—high in the mountains – something that could change the way the human race evolves?"

"Shit!" The pilot slammed his fist onto the control panel. "Nestor Alvarez was either very stupid or very selfish!" He turned to Karl. "And you say that it was strange that the man died? Ha!...I say that it was timely. The man was old and paralyzed. At least he can lie in his grave knowing that he did one useful thing before he died."

"Meaning?" Karl stared stone cold at the mountain peaks.

"Meaning he told me how to find the Spaniard!" Baldock shook his head. "I didn't really need Nestor Alvarez to tell me how to get to the northern peak of Chupiorco. I have a 'GPS' for that."

"Nestor told us more than just how to get to the Spaniard, Dr. Baldock." Crantz shook his head. "We could have spent months searching for the others if Nestor hadn't known about them." The mountaineer rubbed his chin. "What did he call them?...The 'Indian man of the southern peak, the man 'from the Lago' on the east and...'"

He shook his head again. "I didn't understand what he said about the one to the west. The name sounded foreign – something like 'gringo', a European perhaps."

He turned to face the pilot. "But Nestor knew that those three were gone. Lost, he said – the sons lost and the mother's dead...He meant the plants, Dr. Baldock. It's strange—even for the Kallahuaya—to refer to a plant as mother."

"Diego and I had already planned on the Spaniard," Baldock scoffed. "We've done our homework. I knew before the old man spoke his first word that the northern peak is where we wanted to be."

There was a moment of silence.

"High mountains can be very unfriendly, Dr. Baldock." Karl shook his head. "Nestor gave us very precise instructions. He said that the way can change with the days, with the light. The Quechua words he used have no real translation, doctor...He said that, at that altitude, time will have no meaning. Night will become day. The rocks may move and we will not see them. He said that at the top of Chupiorco, rocks are men and men are rocks – the living are dead and the dead are living."

"At the peak, what we would know as normal in our world is different...Very different at the peak of Chupiorco. But the Quechua words said even more than that." He nodded. "Much more...It's...Nestor was trying to tell me of the difficulty – not of the climb...The difficulty of what we are seeking."

The mountaineer stared out the window, a worried look on his face. "Nestor did not have the energy to find the Spanish words and the Quechua – it's not what I understand well."

Baldock shrugged. "I don't mean to say that visiting the old man wasn't interesting, Karl. What he told us may make it easier. Maybe cut a few days off our trip."

The helicopter pitched as a current of air swept through a mountain pass. The aircraft stumbled then grasped the thinning air and slowly descended into a small valley that creased the rock of Chupiorco.

At over fourteen thousand feet, the cloudless sky seemed to float on the mountain, a pale blue drape stretched over rocky ground. Gideon Baldock made it a perfect landing, playing in the gusts and tugging on the blades just enough to bring the aircraft gently down onto the parched soil of an abandoned field of maize. The crop had managed to push its way through the rocky soil but the lack of moisture and the blistering radiation of high altitude had withered the leaves and left the dried stalks matted on the ground.

The dust whipped up by the spin of the helicopter soon disappeared with the rainless squalls that twisted off the mountain.

Chapter Seventeen

"I never knew the name of that small town." The patient shook his head and watched the shadows dance on the window. "It was a desolate place but beautiful – desolate and beautiful." He turned to Marian. "That's an odd combination, don't you think?"

Marian Priest tilted her head. "It can be. I was in the north once. My father was a geologist. He used to be away a lot – on field trips, out in the bush. But one summer he took my mother and me with him. Up past Resolute Bay in the Canadian Arctic."

"I was fourteen – maybe fifteen then and the arctic was the last place in the world I wanted to spend my summer but…" She looked down at her hands, folded on her lap. "I wanted to go back there – with Diggy."

"It was the openness, the vastness, the emptiness…So desolate, so beautiful. And the air—the sky was clear, pale blue as if…As if you were looking through a sheet of translucent paper with an oblique summer sun shining day and night." She nodded. "That was beautiful – desolate and beautiful."

"Yes…That town was just like that. On the west side, the valley dropped away." Karl shook his head.

"You couldn't see the bottom. It was packed full of cloud as thick as smoke never quite...Never quite lifting high enough to reach the village, always letting its moisture fall to the west. That cloud was beautiful too – desolate white and beautiful."

"Perhaps that's where they went. The villagers, I mean. Perhaps they moved down the mountain to where the rain was." He turned away from the window and rubbed his eyes. "There was a church, a very pretty church – sort of a white alabaster, bleached by the sun. It was just above the village, just up the hillside. From the steeple, you could see the houses – huts, really – gray-red mud, dry and crumbling. There was nobody there." He shrugged. "The ground was hard as concrete, packed and split by the heat of the day and the cold of the night."

"There...There were terraces, steep terraces that marched up the mountain, almost farther than you could see but...The terraces had crumbled too." Karl sighed. "And when one of the higher ones broke, it shot its dried rock and sand down taking out the others in its path...I bet that the whole slope is gone by now – worn smooth with time."

Crantz looked at the doctor. "I suppose that's Mother Nature taking back what's hers? The village – even after so many years, was not meant to be there and she punished them. She turned them away."

Marian shook her head. "I'm sure that the people there must have flourished at some point. It takes time to build a town, a church...But I don't understand. Why did you land there, in an abandoned town? You must have needed animals, supplies. Where did-?"

"Well, yes!" Crantz averted her gaze. "There were no people in the town...But the animals...That's right..."

"Florentino had arranged for his people to leave three pack animals – llamas. At the church...They were waiting for us at the church. That's where we were supposed to rest."

"To acclimatize?"

Crantz nodded. "We were already over fourteen thousand feet up and Diego... He had just arrived. He hadn't had time to adjust. But Baldock..." Karl's words trailed away, lost in the dark water of painful memories.

"Baldock..." Marian frowned. "I never met Gideon Baldock. Diego had told me only that the man was well known in his field, that he never did anything without purpose."

Karl Crantz squeezed his eyes closed. "Gideon Baldock is a selfish, egocentric bastard. He's...He's..."

Marian said nothing. She reached over to the small nightstand then handed her patient a tissue to dry the tears.

"Baldock had over a week to adjust and...I...I'm used to the altiplano. But Diego..." Crantz shook his head. "Diego hardly had time to catch his breath. Baldock just wanted to get to the northern peak! That bastard didn't care for anything except his damned seed!"

"Diego started to suffer from altitude?"

The patient nodded. "It began in Chajaya. Diego was exhausted. He couldn't sleep...That happens sometimes when the air you're used to breathing is suddenly only half as thick. It's like...Like you can never quite catch your breath…You can never sigh deep enough."

"We'll rest here today then head up the mountain at dawn." Karl Crantz had packed most of the gear off the chopper and laid the saddlebags and rucksacks on the hard ground at the entry of a small barn. The three llamas grazed on the fresh grass that had been spread across the floor of their stall, the animals oblivious to the newcomers. "It'll give us all a chance to-"

"We leave now." Baldock had been surveying the hillside, his arms folded across his chest as the two others piled the equipment from the aircraft.

"I could use a little…"Diego wheezed and wiped a string of blood-tinged phlegm from his lips.

"We can take advantage of the daylight and set camp before dusk." Baldock ripped open one of the bags and pulled out a down-filled jacket. "And get your coats out. Once we hit the shaded side of the mountain, the temperature drops like a rock."

Diego looked at his uncle. "In the afternoon? It shouldn't-"

"I've climbed Chupiorco only once before, Diego." The mountaineer nodded. "Dr. Baldock is right. There is a glacier on the northwest side – two thousand, maybe twenty-five hundred feet up from here."

"It's surrounded on three sides by wide rocky outcrops that keep the ice in constant shade. That's where we'll need the crampons – to make the traverse then-"

"Then over the top, Crantz."

"Over the top of-?"

"We follow the glacier to where it feeds out from the northern peak. That's where we're going, isn't it?...Look." Baldock pulled out a folded wad from his pack. "I've had a watch on this mountain for the past month. These satellite photographs give us precise readings of the terrain, the pitch of the slope."

He drew a path with his finger. "We can climb the glacier almost all the way to nineteen and a half thousand feet – at least to this point." He tapped on a blurred section of the map.

"And what do you suppose, doctor, is under that cloud cover?" Karl clenched his jaw.

"What does it matter, Karl?! At that point, we'll be less than five hundred feet from the summit, the mountain narrows and that's where we pick up Nestor's path to the Spaniard."

"No! We follow Nestor's directions." Crantz stood up. "It's safer and we know that it's been done before. It's the way Nestor first made it to the top. It's the path Nestor took when he came upon the man."

"I said that we take the glacier, Crantz!" Baldock glared at the mountaineer. "I've paid good money and lots of it for this map and for the experts to look at it. This route will save us at least two days compared to the way that witch doctor said we should go." He shook his head. "I can't waste time and money zigzagging up some rocky hill. Shit! You told me you climb mountains! You're an expert?!"

Crantz was silent for a moment. "I have never been to the top...To the top of Chupiorco, Dr. Baldock. I have been as high as twenty thousand feet but...But the weather forced me back."

"If you reached twenty thousand then you were at the top!"

The mountaineer shook his head. "The maps we have are not always reliable. The peaks of the Cordillera Apolobamba have never been accurately measured. I reached twenty thousand but I was still far from the top...And I never climbed by the glacier."

Baldock threw the map back into his pack and cursed. "Get ready. We'll make first camp at the foot of the ice."

"But my nephew is sick." Crantz motioned at the younger man who was seated in the shade of the barn roof, his head between his knees. "He needs time – a day perhaps."

"I need that boy when we find the plant." Baldock pointed at Diego. "He is the one who will harvest the seed, collect samples of leaf and root – whatever needs to be done. He is as important to me as he is to you. And if he is sick down here, he's going to be sick up there. So the faster we get up and back the better it will be for you, for me and for your damned nephew!"

"And you left that day? You left for the climb even though Diego was sick?" Marian pulled back from the bedside.

"No! No! Uncle Karl..."The patient fell silent. "Diego insisted that we continue."

"He had overheard our conversation and as soon as Baldock mentioned how much he needed Diego at the top…"

"It was as if a surge of energy had hit the boy. He stood up and said that he was fine, that Baldock was right and the sooner we reached the top, the better." Crantz shrugged. "It was an easy climb. I figured we made nearly twenty-five hundred vertical feet that day. We reached the edge of the ice just after dusk and set up camp."

"And my husband?"

"He...He seemed to be fine." Crantz took a deep breath. "The boy stumbled once or twice but I think that was more because of his eyes than symptoms of altitude sickness."

"His eyes?"

The patient nodded. "He told me later that he had had surgery – keratotomies to fix his short-sightedness. With that kind of surgery, once you reach a certain altitude, pressure behind the cornea can build up sometimes and gradually...Very gradually, the climber loses his sight. It all returns, of course, once you return to the bottom but...But Diego didn't tell me...Until we were near the top."

Chapter Eighteen

Diego was the first to awake that morning. In fact, he had slept so little that 'awakening' was not a good description of how he started his day. The night had been a gray haze for the young botanist, the silence of the glacier broken only occasionally by the groans of ancient ice shifting, painfully making its way downhill. No living creature made its home on the icepack. There were no songs of birds, no nattering of small animals that would normally wake a man living in the open.

The icy river had robbed the hillside of its vegetation, stripping the soil and everything that clung to it, sucking in at its edges, pulling in the tiniest plant so that not even a weed could start to put down its roots.

They had tethered the llamas next to the tent but even these animals, accustomed to the cold and the rocky mountains, bleated throughout the night, disturbed by the strange empty desert where they had made camp.

Close to seventeen thousand feet...That's what Karl had said before they had packed into their sleeping bags for the night. That meant another three thousand vertical feet before they reached the top...If the maps were right. And even if they were, finding the plant – finding the Spaniard – might take days.

Diego crawled out of the tent and pulled his down jacket tightly across his shoulders. He rubbed his right thigh – the spot where Baldock had given him the injection the night before. 'Dexamethasone' he had called it. It had made his breathing easier – no more blood in his spit but his eyes were no better. It was if a translucent gray curtain had been pulled across the mountain. Like scanning the rocks of a murky aquarium, he could see outlines, shapes, areas of light and dark but the details, the contours of the terrain were gone, smudged like a child's oily canvas.

The trio had pitched tent on the barren ground at the edge of an anomaly on a strange mountain. Even at seventeen thousand feet, this glacier would not have existed so close to the equator had it not been for the protection afforded by the massifs that rose up on each side of the ice. The rubbled gray-blue stretched across from east to west for nearly half a mile, smooth as glass in spots and jumbled into twisted hills that bordered deep crevasses in others.

At the foot of the frozen river, the ice formed a gently sloping iron-hard plateau, windswept boulders at its margins scattered among crushed rock.

As the glacier rose to the north, its pitch changed and took almost a vertical lift like a waterfall, frozen as it poured over the brim of the northern peak, three miles in the distance.

Nestor's path was supposed to lead across the ice to the western side then downhill again around the crest of the hillside, left at the boulder that looked like a bear, right at the rock whose flat face watched the western sky – turning and twisting until they reached the top of the glacier at the northern peak. But they had decided to follow the route chosen by Gideon Baldock.

The three men pulled down their small camp, loaded up the animals then headed onto the ice. The llamas began to follow an unmarked trail to the west and it was only after twenty minutes of bleating and spitting that Karl was able to force the team onto the upward path straight to the northern peak.

It was while they were loading the animals that Karl first noticed that his nephew wasn't quite right. "You're better this morning, Diego?"

"I feel great!" The younger man answered without looking at his uncle.

"Hungry? That shot Dr. Baldock gave you yesterday can make you hungry – very hungry, sometimes."

"I could eat a horse! Or maybe one of these llamas, if we can't find a horse... When's breakfast?"

"Not for another hour or two. I'll decide once I see how fast we can trek on the ice. We'll break once we're well on our way." He reached into his coat. "Chocolate should tide you over."

Diego stretched his arm towards the blur in his uncle's hand and grasped thin air.

"Here." The older man leaned forwards.

Diego clutched at his uncle's coat then found the prize held between Karl's fingers.

"Is something wrong?"

"It's the glare off the ice, uncle." The young man shaded his brow. "It makes my eyes tear."

Karl glanced at the icepack. The sheen of the glacier sparkled in the early morning light. The sheer brightness of the day rose up from the frozen river but the glare was minimal – no sun in the early morning, no sun ever on this section of the mountain.

"Put these on and don't take them off. Your eyes were very sensitive when we climbed years ago...They haven't changed. These glasses helped then and they'll do the same now."

Twelve hours later, just as the sun sank below the western edge of the mountain, the climbers crested the brim of the glacier and set foot on the base of the northern peak. Over the top, the river of ice narrowed, flattened then climbed in a vertical spiral to the frozen lake at the top of the mountain.

As soon as they had climbed over the edge of the icefall, the climate seemed to change. The stony silence of the glacier gave way to a hollow wind that tore at their bodies and threatened to push the newcomers back over the brink.

The trio braced themselves against the biting gale and began the descent, one by one, off the ice onto the rocky scree at the glacier's edge. In the dusky twilight, halfway down the slope, Diego lost his footing and began to slide.

The patient trembled and pulled the covers over his chest. He squeezed his eyes shut and clenched his teeth together. "It...It was so painful, such...Such agony."

"Is that where he died...My husband? He...He didn't even get to see what...To find what he had traveled all the way to the mountains for?"

"No." Crantz pulled the covers away from his face and gazed at the doctor through the clouds of his cataracts. "Diego didn't die on the glacier. No...He was too...Too brave for that. But the fall down the ice – that changed so much. After the fall..."

The patient stared out the window. An evening wind had begun to stir, buffeting the young buds of a cherry tree, blowing clouds of pink petals onto the glass. "It's a cherry tree, isn't it? Springtime in Seattle – it must be a cherry tree."

Marian nodded.

"I can see that's what it is." Crantz rubbed his eyes with his twisted hands. "I can see it so well now even though I'm nearly blind. But when we were near the top..."

A tear trickled from the corner of his eye. "When we were near the top of Chupiorco, I could see so much better but I could not see that the fall had changed everything... Everything."

"How badly did he suffer?" Marian covered her eyes with her hand. "Was it long for him? Was-?"

"The fall itself wasn't life-threatening. But it was all so preventable...So..."

Crantz shook his head. "I headed down the icefall first. I took the three pack animals with me. That's what I always did – let the animals go first. They would find the easiest trail, the one with the best footholds. But the ice was so smooth with a sheen of melt on the top that greased its surface..."

"The llamas found the way, though. Fifty vertical feet to the rock from the top of the glacier – a pitched slope of a hundred, maybe a hundred and fifty feet." The patient turned his blind stare at the window again. "Diego was next but his eyes were worse in the dimming light. He made it down halfway then a gust of wind seemed to lift him – just lift him right off his feet and throw him down the hill. He tumbled, slid mostly – nearly a hundred feet down the glass – head first into a large boulder."

Marian gasped.

"No, no...Diego was okay. It was like when he fell into the boards playing hockey in high school. Remember? That same year you met? The year he saved you from Youngward?"

"He told you about his broken wrist?" The doctor pursed her lips. "It wasn't an event he liked to talk about."

"Yes...No." Crantz hesitated. "He didn't like to talk about himself very much. But he had to tell me after the fall.

"You see, Diego would have died right there if he hadn't lifted both arms and protected his head. The blow was taken by both wrists – smashed the bones but the worst break was the right wrist because...He said that he had broken it before. That's when he told me about the hockey."

Crantz drew in a deep breath. "When he hit the boulder, the bone tore right through...Right through the skin. It had become dark so fast...So fast..."

"I remember that sudden change – light to dark. It was as if someone had just snuffed out the sun, taken away the light, taken away the hope." He shut his eyes tight.

Marian bent forwards and touched her patient's arm.

Crantz shuddered. "When I reached Diego, I crouched down and I felt a wetness, a warm wetness but...At first I thought that it was just the melt from the ice. Then...The cloud cover opened for one brief moment. And I saw Diego, lying flat on his back, the wind knocked out of his chest. His left arm was trapped beneath him and his right arm...All I can remember is the jagged open bone of his wrist pointing...stabbed into the sky."

"It was as if...As if it were showing us. And in that short glimmer of moonlight, I looked up from the raw end of bone and saw a small light – a campfire, high on the northern peak."

"At first, I thought that he was dead. I thought that he had broken his neck." Crantz bit down on his lower lip. "It was the only time that Baldock seemed to care about anyone else's well-being. I suppose he realized how important Diego was – how important his hands were to the expedition."

"Baldock almost broke his own neck getting down the slope. We pulled Diego away from the edge of the ice and as soon as we did, he regained consciousness."

The patient stared at his doctor. "He was in such pain. I...I could see it in his eyes – even in the dark. But the first thing...The very first thing that Diego did was lift his shattered arm and point...He pointed at the light – at the light of the campfire on the mountain with the open bone of his wrist and then he said...He said, "There he is Uncle Karl. He's waiting for us...The Spaniard of the northern peak is waiting for us."

Silence.

"At that point then...As a botanist – to collect samples, I mean." Marian shook her head. "Diego couldn't have been much use to the expedition. Did he go back?... Back on his own?"

Crantz shook his head. "Your husband was much too stubborn for that. Once he saw that light, once he knew that what we were searching for was almost within reach, he...He refused. He refused my advice, the advice of his uncle."

The patient sighed. "I had to fix his wrists, so that he could manage somehow."

"Baldock pulled on his elbow while I pulled in the opposite direction – on his hand, to straighten the breaks. The night had turned black again. I could hardly see. But I could feel the bone, on the left side, slide back into position and then I wrapped it with some pieces of firewood I had packed in my knapsack."

Karl shuddered. "The right wrist was much more difficult with the bone exposed. The moonlight flickered – like a switch – from behind the clouds. I could just make out the bones…The raw ends were packed with small bits of rock and gravel. But mostly…I couldn't see. I had to feel with my bare hands...I washed the open wound and then Baldock and I pulled just like we did on the other side and Diego...He was...He was brave."

"But the cries, the pain and finally that sucking sound as the broken bone popped back underneath the skin..."

"And then...Then I don't remember much after that." Crantz squeezed his eyes shut. "Diego blacked out and didn't come to until morning."

Karl's chest heaved. "I'm tired and my heart...It...It's started again. It feels as though it wants to jump right out of my chest."

Marian reached over and put her hand on her patient's wrist. She counted the beats. "Your heartbeat…..It's irregular again."

She kept her finger over the pulse. "There. Very irregular for five or six beats then back to sinus rhythm. I'll order another ECG and adjust your medication. It should be better by the morning." She stood up and turned towards the doorway. "You should rest now."

"You'll be back in the morning?"

The doctor shook her head. "Tomorrow is Saturday. One of my colleagues will be doing rounds – Dr. MacDermot. He'll take good care of you."

"But there's more – more to tell about the mountain, about Diego. He said for me to-"

"I'm sorry, Karl." A tired smile creased Marian's face. "I...I want to know everything as much as you seem to want to tell it but...This is the second evening I've spent here with you, away from my family, away from my-"

"You have a family?" The patient's voice quivered.

Marian leaned against the doorframe. "I have...Half a family. I have a son. He's with his grandmother this evening...But he's with me tomorrow."

"A son..." Karl Crantz turned off the bedside light casting a dark shadow over his face. He swallowed hard and took a deep breath. "He is a very lucky man...The father, I mean. To have you as a wife and...And a son."

"My son is almost two years old." Marian shook her head and stared into the half-lit room. "I named him after his father but...He's never known his father. You see, less than two weeks after Diego left, I found out I was pregnant and...It was going to be his big surprise when he came back...A big surprise for Diggy when he came back...But he never did."

The patient's breathing quickened and his voice grew hoarse. He coughed. "Then...He must come to see Diego's uncle, his father's last blood relative. He must come so that I can tell him about his father...About his brave father."

Marian shook her head. "My son is not used to seeing patients with-"

"To see his uncle. He can call me Uncle Karl." The patient's voice was firm. "Please!...To see his uncle!"

The doctor paused. "I suppose I can make rounds myself. He can stay at the nursing station while I see my patients."

"But I must-"

"And I can bring him in for a short visit to see his uncle...His Uncle Karl."

Chapter Nineteen

Marian Priest scanned the pages of the medical chart then sat down at the bedside. She had been in the room for more than twenty minutes and the patient had not stirred from his deep sleep. The twisted fingers of his right hand clutched a small note pad, half-hidden beneath the sheets.

She watched the emaciated figure, counted the shallow breaths as the failing body heaved in a half lung full of air then let it escape between parched lips.

He had slept the whole night through, according to his nurse. Not like the first night on the ward. That first night had been twelve hours of fear and confusion for Karl Crantz.

The doctor had seen it so many times before. Dying patients – mind disconnecting from body...Or body from mind? It seemed that when the physical body began to break down, the mind found itself alone, its partner, its reference point to the world around it, gone.

Loss of contact with reality, confusion, fear. It was if the mind became separate – separate from its dying frame...A preparation for what was to come, perhaps?...And it was always worse at night.

The patient's eyelids fluttered but the rest of his body remained deathly still – except for the hesitant, slightly labored breathing...In and out, a long pause then finally, a gasp and another breath.

Karl appeared thinner today – he seemed to have lost pounds even in the last twelve hours – eyes sunken deeper into the skull; jaw and cheekbones more rough and jutting...Even his hands...

Marian leaned forwards and watched Karl's arms rise and fall with the movement of his chest. The man lay with his left arm uncovered. It was the first time she had been able to examine either hand. He had kept them under the sheets, seldom bringing them above cover, only rarely showing them to the world.

She winced. Useless claws, the fingers mangled by wear, twisted by arthritis. The day before, she had watched him pin the cover between his wrists and pull it over his chest. He was unable to grasp or hold with his fingers. The muscles of his hand were thinned, atrophied. Peripheral nerve injuries, perhaps...And the wrist – the bones were buckled, contorted. Not an arthritic deformity.

She leaned over and tugged the sheet off his right hand. The fingers were the same as on the left. But the wrist was different—a rough, thickened scar creased the back of the wrist and snaked its way halfway up the forearm. She was about to lean across and touch the wound when Crantz moaned and opened his eyes.

He peered at her for a moment then rubbed his eyes with the sheets. The world remained a blur. "Good morning...It is morning, isn't it?"

"Almost ten-thirty." She smiled. "You slept better than the night before."

Karl nodded. "The nurses gave me something – a pill, I think—to help me sleep, to stop the dreams."

"Just a sedative through the intravenous. It's fast and it's effective."

He looked at the tubing that led to the curve of his left elbow. "I...I can't remember anyone putting this in."

"They called me – an hour or two after I left last night." The doctor nodded. "It's not uncommon, when the body starts to weaken. Confusion, the feeling of being lost, alone, hopelessness, helplessness – it's a natural physiological response."

Crantz sighed. "Thanks...At least...At least it made the dreams less vivid, less real."

"Dreams?"

"Dream." The patient closed his eyes. "Just one dream...But it's always the same."

"About what happened on the mountain?" Marian shook her head. "You couldn't have prevented what happened to Diego. The fall down the ice. It was an accident, an accident that can't be changed."

He grimaced. "Not about the fall. Diego...Diego was strong, stronger than I thought he could ever be." He took a deep sigh. "No, the dream is about the Spaniard, the man we met on the northern peak."

"Do you mean Nestor Alvarez?...That...That medicine man was telling you the truth? There really was a man at the top?" Marian Priest pulled her fingers though her hair. "Diego once told me that at high altitude, plant life is limited. Nothing grows, nothing survives above eighteen thousand feet."

Marian paused and looked into her patient's clouded eyes. "Karl, memory can be a strange thing when you're ill. And moments to remember can be distorted by exhaustion, by the thin air. Things can appear-"

"There was a campfire, too. Baldock saw it, I saw it and Diego saw it." The patient stared at his doctor. "And it is next to impossible to have a fire at twenty thousand feet."

There was a moment of silence then Crantz turned, his eyes wide and excited. "Where is he? You said that you would bring him."

"Bring-"

"Your boy! Your son! To see his uncle! You promised that you would bring him – to see his uncle."

"My son is at the nursing station." Marian smiled. "He's on his second popsicle of the morning while I see my patients. He's-"

"Bring him to me!...Please. He's...He's my only blood relative...My nephew's child."

"He hasn't seen many people in your condition, Karl. In a way, I'm-"

"Please, Marian." Karl's lips trembled. "Please. At least for a short visit – just to say hello. Just…Just so I can tell him that his father would be proud, proud of him."

The doctor smiled, turned and left the room.

A moment later, Marian returned, a blond haired boy, eyes wide and deep blue, clutching her finger and hiding behind the wings of her white coat. "Come." She sat down and lifted him onto her lap.

Karl grimaced, twisted his body and sat up, then leaned his back against a small mountain of pillows. He stared at the boy for a moment. "Hello...I...I can barely see you. My...My eyes." He turned to Marian. "His name. You haven't told me his name."

"James…James Crantz." She stroked the curls over the back of her son's head, still buried deep in her breast.

"He hasn't had much experience with people – other than me and my parents."

"James Crantz...A son without a father." The patient stretched out a crippled hand and touched the boy's shoulder. "James?...Say hello? Say hello to your Uncle Karl?"

Marian shook her head. "He doesn't have many words yet. His pediatrician says that-"

"By two years old, a child usually says a few-"

"James is almost eighteen months now." She smiled. "His doctor says that lack of socialization, my hours away...No father... He assures me that it will come, the words will come."

She kissed her son on the cheek and turned him to face the patient. "It will all come when you're ready, won't it James? Do you want to say hello to your Uncle Karl?"

The boy pushed his face deeper into his mother's chest then peeked out at the gnarled hand that lay limp at the bedside. He buried his face again then turned and silently reached out to touch the curiosity covered to the knuckles in white sheet.

Crantz lay motionless, staring through the blur at the child's face and tasseled hair. He felt the soft touch of the boy's hand gently pressing on his wrinkled skin – a probing finger then a firmer grip as James felt along the twisted roller-coaster of his uncle's forefinger, across the crevasses of the palm then, braver now, pushing the sheet over the wrist and stroking the scar on the back of the patient's forearm.

Karl swallowed hard and withdrew his arm beneath the sheets.

"That was a start." Marian smiled. "No words but a thorough physical examination. One of the nurses at the desk twisted her finger yesterday." She ran her fingers through her son's soft hair and kissed him on the cheek.

"You must have been watching me when I wasn't watching you...When I took a look at her finger this morning."

"He's...He's beautiful." Karl wiped the moisture from his eye. "Can you say that about a boy? Can you say that he's beautiful?"

"You can say that...Yes. Every child is beautiful."

"Have you told him about his father? About why... Why Diego could not be with him?"

Marian looked out the window and sighed. "It's been very hard to talk about Diego to anyone up until now, until you arrived. I just...I just didn't know what to tell people – especially James."

She glanced at Crantz then closed her eyes. "Now that I know that there was an end...Closure is a good thing. Now, perhaps, I can tell James about Diego...About how I remember his dad."

"Da!" The child reached out and grabbed the patient's hand beneath the sheet. "Da!"

"Two words now! 'Mama' and 'Da'." She gave her son a hug. "But this is your Uncle Karl, James. Can you say Karl? Uncle Karl?"

Crantz stared at the child. "When I became sick...I had a lot of time...A lot of time to think and...I realize now that when you're young...When you're young you can see everything, Marian... Everything. Shapes, faces, animals – among the leaves of a tree, in the clouds. But when you grow old...It's so hard sometimes. So hard to see these things.....Things that are really there."

The patient turned to his doctor. "Promise me that you'll talk to him about the shapes and the animals in the clouds – the things that adults can't see. Maybe, he can help you keep them longer...Or get them back and maybe...Maybe you'll never be like me...Never grow old."

The room was silent then Crantz whispered, "A child makes even the shortest life worthwhile."

"Your life?"

The patient nodded.

"Some would say that sixty-seven is a long life." The doctor pursed her lips. "I try to stress to my patients that the years you have already experienced can never be taken away. They are your own personal treasures. At this stage-"

"Doctor, when a patient is ninety-nine years old, a lifespan of one hundred seems short."

Marian Priest pursed her lips. She gazed at her patient for a moment then said, "I've been in practice for about two and a half years and that's...That's the first time a patient has said that to me. It's something that I had always thought was true but in my training, we were taught to stress the positive.   But-"

"But tomorrow sometimes is here before you know it."

There was a long pause then Marian nodded. "That's what Diego used to say...That's exactly what he used to say."

The patient winced and closed his eyes tight.

"Karl?" Marian placed her hand on his shoulder. "Karl, are you all right?"

"Fine. I'm fine" He stared out the window. "It's just...What we were talking about."

"About the future? About tomorrow?"

"No! I...I don't want to talk about that...I mean about what we were talking about before—about the dream. The dream is frightening but there's such...Such certainty in it...Every time I have the dream, it's so disturbing and certain...In a strange sort of way."

"Dreams are special, Karl. Each one is our own little work of art. The 'craft of the night'." Marian nodded. "I have a friend who's a psychologist and that's what she calls dreams – the craft of the night."

The patient shook his head then shivered. "My dream is not an art, Marian, not a craft. It's something only the night can bring. I think that mine is something... Something that can be crafted only under a cloak of darkness."

"A dream is not something to be feared. A dream comes from deep inside, Karl." Marian stroked her son's hair. "Many frightening dreams, disturbing dreams are about loss – loss of a loved one or the fear of that loss but often a dream can be very revealing. It can point out your feelings, your thoughts, your perceptions...Very accurate observations that only your subconscious is able to realize."

"You can tell that much from a dream?" Crantz squinted at his doctor.

"Sometimes." Marian let James down onto the floor and he waddled over to the window, padding at the petals that had stuck to the wet surface of the outside. "You said that the Kallahuaya healer was right. There was a man at the top of the mountain."

Crantz nodded. "The dream is about the Spaniard – always about the Spaniard. I've had it so often that sometimes I'm not sure whether what I remember is what really happened or...Maybe what I dream is the truth."

The patient stayed silent.

"So first tell me what you remember – what you remember to be the truth."

The patient coughed hard then swallowed. "After the accident – after his fall, Diego seemed as obsessed with the mountain as Baldock had become. He was unstoppable. It must have been the campfire he saw that night...The fire that could not have existed at such an altitude...But the one we all saw..."

Chapter Twenty
The glacier at Chupiorco

Gideon Baldock had come to the mountain well prepared. Long before the trio had set out on their climb, he had decided that nothing – storm, injury, even death – would stand in the way of his goal. He needed the mountaineer for his skills and knowledge of the region and he needed the botanist for his knowledge of how to properly collect his specimen without killing the plant.

Now that his scientist had been injured, the man's usefulness was diminished but, as a tool, the man need not yet be discarded. Diego still could be helpful – if the plant was as unusual as he expected.

That night, Baldock pumped the young man's body full of narcotic to the point that even with open bony wounds, Diego slept peacefully and silently. But at first light, as the sun cast a pink glow onto the massif of the northern peak, the botanist awoke with a chilling shriek.

"He needs some more!" Baldock prepared the syringe and began to pull open the young man's shirt.

"But it's been less than an hour since the last dose!" Karl grabbed the doctor's arm. "You had said that once every four, maybe every three hours should be enough. At this altitude, he should need less – not more!"

"I'm the doctor here! The man's in pain!" Baldock glared at Crantz. "And I am not going to risk the success of this expedition because of his uncontrollable screams." He pointed at the mountaintop, still covered in wisps of cloud. "You have no idea what it is we are after, do you? I have explained it to you! Diego has explained it to you but... You really have no idea!"

Baldock plunged the needle into Diego's shoulder. "At the top of this mountain is a man – a very old man, Mr. Crantz – who guards the greatest treasure mankind will ever know. Civilization came to this land searching for gold but, if this plant is what I believe it to be, the real Eldorado is waiting for us at the top of that peak." He pulled the syringe out of Diego's arm and pointed the needle at the mountaineer. "And all we have to do...Is take it!"

The doctor stared at his patient as the drug began to take effect. "What if that man – whoever he is – hears us coming? If you knew what he knows, would you give away your secret?" He shook his head. "This will be a fight, Karl. And whoever wins...Takes the prize."

"But we are three, Dr. Baldock. And this man is old. He-"

"Don't be so naive! Do you really believe that we are the first to try to take the plant?" Baldock's words hung for a moment in the thin frost of the morning air. "That witch doctor knew about it. And how many others over the years? Ten? Twenty?...Thousands?" He capped the syringe and pointed the tip of the needle at the peak. "He knows we're coming and he'll be ready."

Baldock leaned over and pulled on Diego's limp body. "We'll strap him to the llama until the morphine wears off and then he'll have to take care of himself."

"We can't take my nephew higher in this condition!" Karl grabbed the young man around the waist. "He must see a doctor! He-"

"I am a doctor!" Baldock pushed the tip of a revolver flush against Karl's temple. "And the doctor says we can leave him here...But I think he would be more useful at the top...I have enough bullets for you and the Spaniard, Karl!"

"Did you tell the police? When you came off the mountain...I mean..." Marian frowned. "To treat anyone like...To do that to Diego..."

The patient ignored the question. "Diego was off the pack animal and moving under his own steam within the hour. It was...Nothing short of amazing." He paused. "But from that point on – until the Spaniard died – your husband's behavior was strange."

"The narcotics?"

"I...I can't recall exactly." Karl shrugged. "He said that he knew where to go and he was talking, always talking. It almost drove Gideon Baldock mad. The man threatened him with the gun at least three times before we reached the top."

"And each time that Diego looked down the barrel of the gun, he just stared and said, 'He's calling us...He's calling us'." The patient shook his head. "Those were the only words that either Baldock or myself could understand."

"Why? Was Diggy delirious? Was it the drugs?"

"Not at all. We stopped several times that day. We were all tired – even the animals...Exhausted.....Except for

Diego." Crantz twisted his hands beneath the sheets. "It seemed that the higher we climbed, the stronger he grew."

"Then what was he saying?"

"Diego's words were only in Spanish – except for the few he spoke to Baldock. But it was a Spanish that I could barely understand. Old words, lost words. But they were words that led us beyond the path that the Kallahuaya had given us. Words that brought us to a cliff face – ninety, a hundred feet straight up...Just as the light disappeared."

Chapter Twenty-One

The steady hum of flowing water greeted her when Marian peeked in to see her patient. She felt guilty that she had been unable to return when she had told him she would. Their Saturday talk had been short. Karl's eyes had started to fill with tears as she left the room. He had turned away when she stopped to ask why. She couldn't bring herself to ask the question. She knew that it was her son that Uncle Karl was crying for.

Even the best plans can change and with her partner sick, it had been up to Dr. Priest to fill in for Dr. MacDermot. Sunday – her time off – had already been a long day. She would return when Karl had finished his shower.

The patient leaned against the edge of the sink. One gnarled hand propped his body against the rail of his walker as he etched words onto the steam of the mirror. The shower was a good distraction. He could sit alone – sit alone and think without the prying eyes and prodding hands that came to check – to check that he was still alive – to check that he was dying on schedule.

The words on the glass faded with the rush of vapor from the showerhead and he traced the lines again...And then again...And then again.

He could feel the words he could barely see – each letter, each line.

Crantz bit hard on his lip and collapsed back onto the seat of his walker. She wasn't coming today! He was just another one of her patients and today...Perhaps Marian didn't really care what had happened to her husband. And the old man could never tell...Never really tell her the truth.

The patient stood back up and traced the words one more time. He choked on the tears, let out a yell then brought both hands crashing down onto the glass.

The mirror splintered and Crantz fell to the floor, the shadows of his vision extinguished by the curtain of blood that oozed from his forehead.

As she stepped back from the doorway, the unmistakable sound of shattered glass pierced into the empty room. Marian Priest opened the unlocked door and tugged on the emergency call button on the bathroom wall. "Karl!" She knelt down and pulled open an eyelid. "Can you hear me?!"

The patient groaned then smiled. "Yes...You're back. Thank you for coming back. I-"

She placed her fingers on his trembling lips and nodded at the two nurses. "He must have slipped. He'll need some stitches." She stared at Karl's twisted hands, small flecks of blood on the underside of each fist. "I can do that here—in the bed."

Marian stood up and watched the patient walk back to the bedside in the arms of an orderly. She turned and looked at the mirror. It had fractured where the two fists had struck their blows, one at the top, the other at the bottom, leaving an isthmus of glass across the middle, ghosts of steam lifting away the words.

She drew closer and mouthed the verse just as the last ghost disappeared:

> Death and Sweet Life
> One sorrow, one bliss
> Each one denied...

The patient had been especially agitated following the accident. It wasn't the loss of blood or the fall. Marian could see that neither had been severe. But Karl Crantz seemed fearful, worried – pleased to see his doctor but, at the same time, apprehensive, as though he wanted to hide.

That was why she made sure that the sterile drape that protected the gash across her patient's forehead while she stitched the wound, fell over his eyes. It gave him a privacy, a calming darkness.

"So. That was quite a tumble you took. Was the floor wet?" The doctor pressed gently on the wound giving a few moments for the numbing effects of the local anesthetic to take hold. She felt a jagged edge and pulled out a shard of glass.

The patient nodded a response.

"Now don't move, Karl. There are still a few pieces of glass here." She sighed. "You're lucky you didn't get it in the eyes."

"I...I can't see a damned thing anyway!"

Marian gave the cut another dab of antiseptic and began to sew the edges together. "It's strange. My son – James... He couldn't stop talking about the man he met yesterday. He-"

"Your son can't talk."

The doctor continued to sew. "Perhaps talking isn't the right word. But he certainly was getting his ideas across. I have never seen him so...So excited." She paused. "He calls you 'Da'."

There was no response from beneath the drape.

"James used the term twenty, maybe thirty times – all day long...His grandmother thought I should tell you that my son...My son seems to have a special...A special affection for you. ...She thought you would like to know that."

The drape began to shake – a soft, steady vibration, the sweet touch of raindrops on parched soil.

"Karl!" She touched his covered face with her gloved hand. "Does what I say upset you?"

"No...I only wish that I could see him. I mean really see him, Marian! Everything...Everything is just a shadow. But when he was here, I could feel him and I could tell so much from his touch...Just from his touch!"

Crantz let out a shaky sigh. "I never married. And now I regret...I regret not having a son of my own."

Marian Priest let the tears subside then said, "Now is not the time to start feeling regrets, Karl. Now is the time to be thankful for all the things you have had – the mountains, the air, the freedom you felt each time that you scaled a peak."

Silence.

"Millions envy the life you have lived."

Still no response.

"We've talked quite a bit over the past few days. I feel..." Marian Priest leaned back, her suture in hand.

"I feel that, even though it's been only a few days, I know you. In many ways you are a lot like Diggy."

The drape began to tremble again.

"And I find that...I find that very perplexing."

"I'm his uncle. There's no mystery in that." The words were clipped and whispered.

"I meant that you seem much like my husband but...He wouldn't be doing what you are doing."

"I don't understand...Diego told me to let you know-"

"Diego would have answered my question." She stabbed her needle into a gauze and peeled open another stitch.

"Your question?"

"When we first met, when I took you on as a patient, I asked you what happened to him, what happened to my husband." She closed her eyes. "It's been a long story, a painful story but...I just want to know what happened, that he didn't suffer. Can you tell me that, Karl? Can you make the story short? Can you bring it to an end?"

The doctor had finished her work and she pulled the drape away from the patient's face. "Can you tell me the end?"

Karl Crantz turned his blind eyes away and stared at the light from the window. "I don't want it to end, Marian...I don't want the story to end."

"Turn your head...And lift." The doctor began to wrap a gauze across the patient's laceration and around his head, like a half-wound turban. "There! Can you see better now?"

Crantz shrugged. "My eyes were pretty useless before I cut myself. I don't suppose that they can be any better now."

"Your eyes were good enough to write on the mirror before you decided to break it with your fists, Karl!" Marian dabbed the dry specks of blood off her patient's hands.

He turned back to face the window.

"And what do those words mean? 'Death and sweet life, one sorrow, one bliss. Each one denied...' "

Marian touched him on the chin. "Whose words are those, Karl? Where do those words come from?"

"They're my words!" Karl's hollow eyes closed then stared back through the clouds of his cataracts. "I write poetry. I write verse. Even when I can't see the words, Marian, I can still feel them! It helps me. It helps me to try and understand."

"But those words." She shook her head. "I'm not someone who has read a lot of poetry but I've seen something like them – something in the same vein...Where do they come from?"

"They come from a dying man, doctor!" Crantz sighed. "They come from a dying man...A dying man who doesn't want the story to end."

Chapter Twenty-Two
The Next Day

The patient gasped, caught unawares when his doctor entered the room. "I thought that you wouldn't come back. I thought that after yesterday...You wouldn't want me as a patient anymore."

Marian Priest sat down and sipped her coffee from a styrofoam cup. "After you kicked me out-"

"I didn't kick you out."

"You asked me to leave. You had to rest. Remember?" She stared at Crantz. "A dying man who didn't want the story to end."

"I was upset. I didn't really want you to go." He looked out the window. "I was afraid you wouldn't come back."

There was a pause then Marian said, "I decided that you were right. You are the one who is sick and...If you can tell me the story, Karl, I can make sure that it won't end. That your story, Diggy's story, will be with me...And with James."

She crossed her legs and smiled. "So...Now I've come to hear the story. To hear you tell the story – the way you want to tell it – fast, slow...Any way you want."

Crantz nodded. "I know that that is what Diego would want, Marian."

"You and Diggy...And Baldock had come to a cliff face-"

"Yes! And nowhere to go. That's where we set up camp that night – stuck in a dead-end, carved into the granite of the mountain." He shook his head. "Except for the rope ladder that we found the next morning...Someone had lowered it while we slept."

The three men stared at the twine and leather that snaked down the rock face directly above their campsite. No one had awoke. There had been no sound that night but the ladder had not been there when they had arrived less than eight hours before – they all agreed on that.

There was a hoist, too – a type of sling fashioned out of animal skins attached to the bottom of the ladder, a way to pull up supplies, a way to lift an injured man to the top of the granite cliff. It was the sling that they used to take Diego to the top.

They had argued about the animals but, in the end, they had decided to let the llamas go. Baldock said that they would be no more than a day at the top but Karl wasn't so sure. It had been the only argument with Baldock that Crantz had won, one of the last the two men were to have.

Diego didn't say anything about the animals. He seemed detached, his thoughts somewhere else, his eyes fixed on the final hill above them. Perhaps it was the pain from his broken arms – perhaps it was the effect of the narcotics. He stayed silent the rest of the way but his body plodded on, oblivious to the cold, unaffected now by the altitude and the thin air.

At midday, just as the sun crested the peak behind a shadow of high cloud, Diego raised both arms above his head and whispered, "We have arrived."

The trio found themselves at the edge of the massif. On the right, a rocky scree led up to an icy peak and, on the left, the mountain fell away thousands of feet through a haze of clouds. And everything was silent – the wind had stopped, not a movement of air. Even the sound of their boots on the rocky ground was muted, as if sound was sacrilegious, an affront to a solemn rite.

Directly in front of them was a narrow alcove, no larger than the stone hut where Nestor Alvarez, the Kallahuaya had spoken his words and where the Kallahuaya had subsequently died. Three sides of the room were shut in by rock and the fourth side – the north side—allowed a small opening that had been half filled in with rubble.

The noontime rays of light shone through the narrow hole and lit the interior walls with a dull glow centered on the twisted form of a small tree. It stood less than five feet in height, a gnarled old woman with a thickened waist. Pale green leafy hands perched on spindly arms reached out and stroked the ground, littered with dung.

At her top, two thin branches, sparsely adorned by wider, scaly leaves- each leaf the color of smudged emerald on ghostly pallor—stretched forwards in an angelic embrace with the cold, empty air.

A sink sized bowl rested at her feet, filled with half melted ice and more dung – her drinking water, her nourishment.

Gideon Baldock was the first through the cleft in the wall. He kicked at the rubble that filled the doorway then pulled the rocks to the side like a swimmer surging for the end of the pool. He scrambled over the last stones then fell into the small chamber.

There was an unfamiliar warmth that filled the rocky cell – a gentle heat, constant and uniform. The three men had felt the change when they stepped through the opening – a vertical thermocline, the cold of the day outside, a mother's warmth within.

Baldock knelt next to the plant. His hand trembled as he reached out and touched the closest leaf. The flat surface shivered in rhythm with its visitor then Baldock placed his flat palm across its spade-shaped surface. The leaf and hand clasped one another – palm in leaf, a perfect fit.

"We...We must take some samples. Diego! A sample! This is why you're here!"

The botanist crouched beside the doctor and fumbled with his splinted arms.

"Give it to me!" Baldock grabbed the sack and emptied its contents onto the rocky floor. "Now, what? What do we need?"

"A leaf. One healthy leaf with its stem. Then press it – but carefully so that it doesn't crease. Place it into the press and secure it."

Baldock clipped the leaf he had caressed and slipped the specimen into the book-like press.

"And a scraping of the bark. A full thickness sample if you can – without harming the plant, I mean." Diego edged closer. "She looks...She looks so delicate."

Baldock grabbed a small knife from the kit. The blade fell into the plant and, as it did, the leaves began to tremble again and a green film oozed from the wound. He carved a square of thick, gray skin then dropped it into a jar.

"And a seed – at least two. Three or four if we can get them." Diego leaned forwards and peered up under the small forest of leaves. "Sometimes, with cold weather plants, the fruit is hidden, protected under the foliage but..." He shook his head. "None here. Perhaps it's the wrong time of year."

"I don't think so, Diego." Baldock was inspecting the water bowl. The snow that had filled it had almost melted, creating a dung soup that was warming in the air of the protected chamber. He stroked the ground with the tip of his boot, scattering a pile of empty shells across the room. "Whoever lives here has had plenty of seeds."

"Please!...Don't harm her." A gentle voice echoed in the small room.

The trio turned to see a crouched figure cloaked in gray, perched on the remains of the rocky barrier that had closed off the room, his gaunt legs unmoving like the strong trunks of an old tree. He spoke again but only Diego could understand.

"We mean no harm, senor." Diego pointed to the specimen bottle. "We only mean to study."

Uncle Karl stood perplexed. He turned to his nephew. "What are you saying? How-?"

Diego's eyes were glazed. "I speak to him in Spanish. He-"

"That is not Spanish!"

"It is an old Spanish, uncle. And, somehow...It comes to me." The botanist turned back to the newcomer. "We come to study and learn...We come to-"

"No! She is to be respected—not studied! She is to be loved – not examined." The man stood up and stepped off the rocks. The hood that had covered his head fell back allowing a shock of black hair to spread across his shoulder.

His dark eyes closed shut and a tear rolled down his face. The single drop slid along the edge of his nose then crept across the crevassed skin of his cheek, slowly tumbling over ridges made smooth by an overlying layer of new growth – a young man clinging to the scaffold of an old frame.

"Ask him who he is! How did he get here?" Baldock grabbed Diego by the shoulder.

The man shrugged. "My name has been lost. My life has been here." He motioned at the tree. "With the mother, the master. She cares for me and I care for her." He sighed. "I came with Pizarro. I came with the conquistadors."

Silence. The last word was understood even by Gideon Baldock.

"Tell him, Diego...Tell him that we need some seeds. We need-"

The Spaniard shook his head. "Only the mother can give her seed and she gives it only to the one who will keep her."

"Then YOU give it to me!" Baldock pulled his revolver and cocked the trigger.

The Spaniard stared at Baldock but did not move. He stood still as a mountain, unmoving as the trunk of an old tree on a windless slope. After a moment he said, "You are the one sent by the healer?"

"Si." Diego answered for Gideon Baldock.

The man smiled, turned and disappeared through the cleft in the wall.

"Come on!" Baldock snickered. "At least the bastard knows what a gun looks like. Now we'll get our seeds."

When the three men came out into the alcove, the Spaniard was gone. The silence of the stone walls had changed and echoed now with a wind that sighed then spat out its breath straight to the back of the stone chamber. The blue sky had clouded and a spittle of rain had moistened the granite.

They found him fifty yards down the slope, perched on a large boulder – like a lonely tree, leaning over the steep drop to the valley floor—but this time his body swayed like a young sapling buffeted by the gusts, yielding to nature's desires.

Baldock approached him and shouted. The words were snatched away by the wind then Baldock began to yell. He stepped closer and as he did, the Spaniard rose from his crouch and struck with a long sword. The gun flew out of Baldock's hand and dropped into the emptiness of the valley below.

Baldock shrieked and the Spaniard stood to his full height. The drizzle had turned into a flood and the wind screamed. They could barely make out the shape of the man – long thin legs and emaciated arms, chest covered with ancient armor and crown topped with Spanish helmet.

Gideon Baldock had fallen to his knees, his wrist dripping red. Diego and his uncle stepped forwards but Baldock was already up. He rushed headlong and threw his weight against the Spaniard's knees. The man's body buckled, the helmet dropped to the ground, the two trunks crumpled, and the tree disappeared over the bluff.

"And that's the dream I keep on having, Marian. The one..."

"The one you said keeps on coming back." She nodded. "It's about the man who died."

"No...I mean yes." The patient sighed. "Baldock killed the Spaniard...At least that's what he intended. He pushed him off the cliff."

"Murder."

"I suppose it is murder – if that was the intent." Karl Crantz turned his gaze towards the window. "Baldock seemed to think that he had killed the man. The bastard gloated for hours! But..." He turned back to Marian. "Diego and I saw it differently. In my dream..."

Marian was silent.

"Do you understand what I'm saying?"

The doctor cleared her throat. "I...I can't believe that Diego would say it wasn't murder if it wasn't. I-"

"No! That's not what I mean! The Spaniard jumped! Baldock barely touched him!" The patient clutched at his chest. "Don't you see, Marian? He knew we were coming. The man wanted to die!"

"We scrambled to the edge of the cliff and I saw him, his body almost floating like a leaf, down and down...Until he disappeared through the cloud. And then it all stopped."

"What stopped?"

"The wind, Marian! Everything stopped. Everything changed back to what it had been like when we first set foot at the top. Our voices, the scrape of our boots on the rock. "

"Just like that!" The patient patted his hands together beneath the sheets.

"It stopped as soon as the Spaniard disappeared." Karl covered his face with the blanket.

"Did you find any seeds? Did you find where the Spaniard kept them?"

The patient shook his head. "He didn't keep any. He didn't store them – he didn't have to. She produced for him whenever he had the need."

Marian cocked her head to the side. "What do you-"

"Baldock sensed that! Somehow, he knew!" Crantz stared at her. "Baldock and Karl...Baldock and I – he hated me! We almost had it out right there...The Spaniard! He was our only chance to get a seed. But Baldock knew."

"He knew?"

Crantz nodded. "Baldock refused to fight. He even refused to answer me. He just turned away and ran back into the cave and...And there she was!"

Chapter Twenty-Three

By the time Diego and his uncle had caught up with Gideon Baldock, the doctor was on his knees, crouched low at the base of the small tree. He motioned for Diego to approach then pointed to the thickened ball of green that had formed beneath the lowest branches. Deep in the heart of the leafy womb, a single seed – clean and fresh, the same size that Baldock had brought with him to Kew – floated in a shallow pool of gray-green fluid.

Baldock looked at Diego's broken arms. "Do I just take it? Grab it with my fingers?"

"It shouldn't make a difference." Diego shook his head. "Any contaminants on your fingers shouldn't matter to the inside of the nut. Yes...With your fingers."

Gideon Baldock reached forwards and touched the turbid water. He groaned and jerked back his hand. The tips of his two fingers, immersed in the liquid, had been scraped clean of their outer layer of skin.

A pungent, acidic odor wafted through the small chamber. Baldock cursed and plunged his hand into the ice water next to the plant.

Diego looked back under the tree but the green sphere had disappeared, tucked back into the bark of its mother.

They made camp in the alcove late that evening. The skies had remained silent since the death of the Spaniard and the stars glittered with the brilliance of the cold, still air. The three men talked long into the night. There was a seed – all three had seen it, tucked into the protective pouch of its mother. But would its retrieval jeopardize the tree itself? Cutting out a seed—maybe its only seed – would there be any more? Or would that surgical wound be the final blow to the plant's precarious existence?

But there was never a need to make a decision. The mother plant had already made it for them.

Diego was the first to awake and the first to go back into the old lady's chamber.

The sun had not yet crested the eastern horizon but its rays had already lit the sky into a crimson fire. The small cleft in the wall would not allow in light until past mid-morning and once in the cave, the botanist had to rely on the synthetic glow of his flashlight.

It seemed an insult, so unnatural, so foreign to expose this plant to such a thing – a being that had lived so long with just the natural world around her, unchanging days to nights, light to dark.

He balanced the light between his splinted arms and then he saw the cluster of fruit that hung from the nearest branch. Four small seeds, dangling at the end of a leafless claw that stretched towards him – an offering as if to say, 'Here I am...I am yours...'

Diego jumped to his feet, crawled back through the cleft and yelled at the others. Baldock pushed his way past and knelt at the trunk of the plant.

"It was the strangest thing." Karl glanced at his doctor.

"I watched Gideon Baldock. He stayed there on his knees for five, maybe ten minutes – staring at the seeds, saying nothing. It was...It was like some sort of religious experience he was having...A...A trance. We both tried to talk to him, Diego and I but...All he would do was mutter words like 'beautiful', 'priceless', 'gift' – he kept on calling it a gift."

"And then, he reached for the seeds, grabbed all four with his injured fingers and spent the next few minutes sitting next to the tree, rolling the nuts between his palms, across his lips, his eyes closed – just...Just touching them."

The patient sighed. "I realize now that it was at that moment.....At that very moment that Baldock decided to...To kill Diego."

"We have our specimens!" Baldock held up the small branch he had teased from the tree, a grape-like cluster of four. "More than the one or two we need. Right, Diego?"

The botanist nodded.

"Then who wants to be the first?" The doctor looked each man in the eye. "Who wants to be the first to bring the greatest discovery of the twenty-first century home? To be the man known as the one who can demonstrate history's momentous event? Who wants to be the one?...Who wants to dance alone at the top of the world?"

No answer.

Karl Crantz shook his head, cursed and left through the cleft in the wall.

Baldock placed two seeds on a flat rock and brought a stone crashing down onto the pair. He lifted the soft, gray-green meat of the nuts to his lips and pulled in the acrid aroma through widened nostrils. With his eyes still closed, Baldock placed the larger of the two kernels on the tip of his tongue and swallowed.

The doctor's body swayed but his eyes stayed shut. Within moments, his chest began to heave and his breathing became shallow, irregular. His back arched and he fell across the ice bucket, spilling the water across the floor.

Diego called out to his uncle and rushed to Baldock's side. He lifted the doctor's head off the stone floor and placed his fingers under his chin, counting the beats of his heart – regular, steady.

Suddenly Baldock's arm reeled up and struck the botanist square in the face. Diego's head whipped back against the wall and he collapsed to the floor. The last thing Diego remembered was the sensation of a hand forcing a small rock—a seed—deep into the back of his throat.

Chapter Twenty-Four

Marian Priest stared in silence at her patient. The man had stopped his story—once again without an ending. "Do you mean Baldock choked Diego? Choked him with the seed?"

Crantz shook his head. "In...In a way, he did. But..." He turned his gaze to the window and the cherry tree. "You see, Marian...The effects of that seed from the top of Chupiorco – Diego called it the 'Judas Kiss'...That cherry tree is a lot like the effects of the 'Judas Kiss'."

"That's an odd metaphor. Why-?"

"No! Not a metaphor! I said that the effects are like the 'Judas Kiss'...A simile."

He motioned with his left hand above the sheets. "You see...The body, the trunk, the branches of the cherry tree live on but the blossoms – the beautiful parts – the beautiful parts fall away and die. And that's what it's like with the 'Judas Kiss'."

"The man who takes the seed...His body lives on – forever, perhaps—but the being, the individual, the person who was once a thing, a real living thing...The beautiful part falls away. He becomes...Taken up and cast away both at the same time. It's as if the man and the plant become one." He shook his head. "The mother consumes the child!"

The patient sighed. "Now that's a metaphor! 'The mother consumes the child'." He turned back to face his doctor. "Never trust a man who speaks in metaphor, Marian. A man once told me that."

"That's what Diego used to say." Marian shifted in her seat. "Never trust a man who speaks in metaphor. It was...It was Professor Turnbull at Kew who used to say that all the time. It-"

"Maybe that's where I heard it! Yes! From Diego, I mean." Karl nodded blindly at the window. "It was Diego who told me about metaphor...Diego...The professor and the metaphor."

Marian stared at the dying man but said nothing.

The patient held his fist to his chest and winced. "I can feel it." He choked. "I can feel it pounding again, Marian."

The doctor felt his pulse. "Very irregular. I'll..." She moved to get up then stopped, her hand still on his wrist. "It's better now." She counted the beats silently.

Crantz nodded. "Yes...For a moment I thought that..."

"Thought that you were going to die?"

"Yes." His voice was barely audible.

A gust of wind spattered pink blossoms across the window. Karl turned towards the sound. "I can just make out the shadows on the glass – the blossoms, the beautiful parts."

He turned back to the doctor. "I found Diego hours later. I just couldn't be inside...I had to think. When I did decide to go back to the cave, Baldock was gone. I had left because what he wanted – taking the seed himself...It disgusted me – the man himself disgusted me!"

"I found Diego. He was hurt. He was barely breathing and his body was cold...As cold as ice."

It was early evening when Karl Crantz wrapped his nephew in a blanket and took him out into the dying light of day. The last rays of sun peaked around the corner of the alcove and warmed Diego's face.

The young man opened his eyes and shuddered. "Baldock...Where's Baldock?"

"Gone, Diego." Karl took off his own coat and placed it around his nephew's shivering body.

"Do you have them?" Diego's eyes seemed blank, empty. "Do you have the seeds, Uncle Karl?"

"Forget the damned seeds! Baldock took them. He's gone with the rest. Halfway down the mountain by now!"

Diego shook his head. "Not all of them!...He pushed one into me." He gagged. "Baldock forced one into my throat – into my gut. I can feel something there, uncle!" He placed a hand on his stomach. "Something that's growing, something that's changing... Something that's changing me?!"

"Let's get the hell out of here!" Karl lifted his nephew under the arms and the two began the long walk back to the ladder.

By the time the two men finally reached the cliff edge, the night had turned black—moonless with high wisps of cloud blocking out the shrouded twinkle of frosty stars. The ladder lay strewn across the top of the bluff. Baldock was still on the peak – no sign of any attempt to get to the bottom.

Why had he not left? He had his seeds. The man could find his own way back down the mountain. Karl felt a shiver, a stabbing cold pierce his chest.

The mountaineer knelt next to his nephew. He had laid Diego down directly onto the hoist when they had reached the cliff face and the young man had immediately fallen asleep. But it was an odd sleep, a disturbed sleep.

He pulled a flashlight from his coat and shone the beam across Diego's face but the face had changed. The skin of the young man's cheeks was stretched and parchment thin. His lips had creased and cracked. And the glitter of youth that used to reflect from his eyes shone back dark and opaque from under half-closed eyelids.

Karl strapped his nephew into the hoist and began to lower him down the cliff face.

It had been difficult for Karl and Baldock to bring Diego up the rock wall. Now, alone, the older man strained against the dead weight as he eased his nephew to the bottom.

Karl paused with half of the rope ladder fed over the edge and braced his shoulder against a boulder. It was at that moment he noticed the subtle flash of metal from the corner of his eye then the scrape of a blade against stone. He turned and caught Baldock's arm, the Spaniard's sword about to come down on his head.

The razor edge shrieked against the boulder and Karl fell forwards away from the rope. The twine purred along the ground and he grabbed the cord, the momentum hauling his frame across the bluff to the edge of the cliff. He strained against the load...Then the Spanish sword came crashing down again.

"You were lucky he missed." Marian pursed her lips. "Baldock seemed a madman before he started and he only got worse. But how did you...?"

"He missed me." Crantz nodded. "I fell...Right over the edge. See?" He held up his twisted arms. "Broke both on impact. I suppose I was-"

"You fell a hundred feet, Karl. In the dark...Head first?"

The patient nodded and turned his face away. "I was lucky...Very lucky."

Marian was silent. She walked over to the window, directly in line of Karl's view. "And my husband?...Is that when he died?"

Karl buried his face in his hands. "Marian...I don't know how to tell you how...What the end was like."

"And how did you get to the bottom of Chupiorco?"

"The llamas...One llama." He kept his face covered. "I found the animal the next morning – when I regained consciousness. And I just let it take me back – back to the village."

Crantz shook his head. "I can't remember much. Just getting onto the animal then waking up in the straw on the barn floor next to the church – the church in the village where we started."

"And you can't remember anything else. How you got there, how many days?"

"Nothing." Crantz shook his head again. "Just the church...That's where I stayed – with Florentino."

"The Kallahuaya healer?"

He nodded. "I don't know how he got there...Or if he was waiting, knew I was coming."

"And what about Diggy's body? Did anyone bury him? Two years...Did you try to go back?"

"I couldn't. I...I told Florentino. I told him everything but he wasn't interested. By myself..." He shook his head. "I was already getting sicker, weaker."

The doctor had turned her back and stood with her arms crossed, staring out the window.

"I think I've figured out how it works. How the 'Judas Kiss' keeps its man alive."

Marian kept her back to the patient and did not respond.

"It's an imprint. The plant takes a specimen of the newcomer – that was from Baldock, his fingers – and creates a seed that recognizes his genetic material...Only his."

The doctor shifted her stance and stayed with her back turned, silent.

"And then some mechanism – telomere reconstitution, perhaps – a rejuvenation of her new man's cells." Crantz coughed. "The seed, as long as he keeps on ingesting it, will keep Baldock alive. And...And the mother plant will produce the seed as long as he feeds her and takes care of her. It's...It's a true symbiosis."

Still no response.

"And the seed won't work for anyone else because..." Karl's voice strained, wanting, desperate. "...Because she can only have one man. She can only produce for one and if another were to find her..." He began to shake. "So the seed will do away with anyone else...The seed will deny them sweet, eternal life."

He stopped suddenly then whispered, "And she'll deny so much…so much more."

Marian held her hand to her forehead and bit down on her lip.

"The Kallahuaya say that there is no such thing as immortality." Karl's hands were now in a violent tremor.

"Florentino...He said that what the Spaniard did, centuries ago and...And what Gideon Baldock did...It isn't immortality that they achieved. They just...They just put their souls on ice. That's why the Spaniard wanted to give his place up...That's why he jumped. He realized. He finally realized-"

The doctor turned and her face was in tears. "Karl! I don't know what to believe anymore! You've...You've told me so many things with so little certainty... Such...Such imprecision, no closure. You have purposely avoided saying the words...You dance around the question when I ask how or where my husband died."

"And now!" She held up her hand. "Now you spew out this...This pseudoscience about how this plant...This...This thing that keeps a man alive forever! How can you, an uneducated man – a man who has spent most of his adult life climbing mountains in the middle of nowhere even pretend to know how such a thing is possible?"

"Who told you, Karl?! Who could have told you about telomeres, about immortality, about imprinting?!"

"It was..." The patient coughed. "It was Diego...Diego explained things to me."

"When? As you carried him across the bluff?! As you lowered him down the cliff?!"

The patient winced and put his hand to his chest. "Please don't, Marian. Whenever I feel that you want to leave...My heart starts to skip." He gasped then swallowed hard. "Oh shit! It's going to jump out of my chest!"

The doctor turned to leave.

"Marian! Please! Don't go! I need to talk to you! I want to-"

She turned back. "I'm going to get the nurse. We need to set up a monitor. The irregularity of your heart is not good. It's unpredictable and hasn't responded to the medication. A twenty-four hour monitor may help – show us what's happening."

She returned in a few moments with a technician who proceeded to hook the patient up with sticky tapes across his chest then plugged him into the wall. A gentle beat, pulses on the screen and pings in the room.

"Back to normal again." The doctor pressed a button and a short strip of paper fed out of the monitor. She studied it quickly then crumpled it up. "Nothing new there. This will record every beat, Karl. I'll ask one of the heart specialists to take a look when we have the twenty-four hour strip."

"I need to talk!" The patient stared at his doctor. "Will you stay?...For a while longer?"

Marian looked at the window then back at her patient. "I'm sorry...Sorry for getting upset." She nodded. "What would you like to talk about?"

"About dying...About leaving everything, everyone I've known and loved." He twisted his hands together. "And about not being able to say good-bye because..."

"I understand." Marian sat down on the edge of the bed. "I've had to deal with this before...It comes with the job."

"I would like to talk to you more as a friend, Marian. Not as a doctor – I need you to talk to me as my...My best and my only friend."

The doctor gazed at the man for a moment then nodded again.

"Thank you." Karl touched her arm with his withered hand then slid it down to rest in her palm. "Florentino called the life we live in this world 'a cocoon'. He believes that death is the process of waking up, of unwrapping that cocoon and flying free – just like a butterfly – by dying, the soul is set free." He nodded. "That's...That's what the Kallahuaya believe."

He sighed and turned his gaze towards the window. Patchy shadows of cherry petals were smeared across the glass once again, pasted on by the rain that had just given way to a brief moment of sunlight. "Florentino did all he could. He tried for nearly two years. That's...That's why I couldn't come out, send back word. There were days when my condition improved but then, a few days later, the world would collapse again."

"He didn't try to get you to a doctor – a medical doctor?"

"In that part of the country, there are no doctors. And to try to get me out..." He stared at the foot of the bed. "Remember how dry that village was? Abandoned, cracked?"

"Desolate but beautiful, you said."

Karl nodded. "But everything had changed – the Spaniard, Baldock...Diego. There are huge gaps, Marian. Days, weeks that I can't remember but I know one thing. It rained. It rained in that village as if to make up for the times that it hadn't. It rained as if the sky was shedding tears for all the months, the years that it had been too selfish…Too selfish to cry."

"The ground turned to mud, the hills began to slide. We had to abandon the church one night. I thought that the whole mountain was coming into my room. A huge crash then dirt pushing through the door!" Karl shuddered.

"But the weather wasn't the only reason we couldn't leave. My arms…" Crantz held up his two twisted sticks. "Florentino applied a salve and bathed the wounds. The breaks healed in less than two weeks. But then my eyes started to grow cloudy and then all the joints in my body seemed to catch on fire. And Florentino fixed that too. But that didn't last…Things turned worse when the cough started."

"And what did this healer do for you then?"

"Florentino described it as life speeding up. He said that something…Something inside had changed and that I was growing old faster than I had before. And, in my body…" He fingered his left upper chest. "In my body, there was a woman – that's what he called it, a woman—who was eating me from the inside."

Karl looked up at Marian. "I know now that what he meant was the cancer. And when I finally arrived here, that's what the x-ray showed – the tumor in my left lung."

There was a long silence then Karl sighed. "I'm doing it again, aren't I?"

"Doing what?"

"I'm straying from the subject. I said that I wanted to talk about dying but now I'm back to what happened on the mountain."

Marian shrugged. "I'm a good listener."

"Thanks." His lips parted into a faint smile.

"Do you think that what Florentino said is true, Marian. Do you think that life is a just a cocoon...And that death can change us into the butterfly?"

The doctor placed her chin in the cup of her hand. "That sounds like a religious question and I'm not a religious person but I do think...I really do think that there is something to that—to the belief of life after death."

The patient stared at his doctor. "You believe that there is a butterfly?"

"I believe that death as the step into blackness, as the end of life makes no sense – it contradicts everything we know." She opened her hands wide. "If you look around you, everywhere you look, everything you see changes but never disappears. Nothing ever really steps into blackness. It just changes."

"And that's what I believe dying is all about too." She nodded. "Death is a change. It's a process – a part of a process, really. Because without death, there can't be any life. In our way of thinking, the two states of being are opposites – one defines the other."

Karl smiled. "That's what Florentino said. Without death, there can be no life. That's why I said that Baldock put his soul on ice and the Spaniard had done the same until he jumped." He nodded. "'Soul on ice' – those are Florentino's words...Death is the liberation of the soul."

"But, in the end, Marian." Karl squeezed her hand and closed his eyes tight. "In the end, I don't really care about the liberation of my soul." His voice sank to a whisper. "I'm scared...I'm so scared...I don't want to die."

Marian clutched her patient's hand and whispered, "You're brave, Karl. And it's your fear that allows you to be that way. Just like Diggy...Just like Diggy."

Karl nodded and shut his eyes tight.

Chapter Twenty-Five

Marian Priest had rushed home as soon as her patient had fallen asleep. It had been sweet bliss for Karl, she was sure, when the tears finally gave way to exhaustion, to the peace of unconsciousness.

She rifled through the old shoeboxes – letters, memos, notes left by Diggy saying he would be back to the apartment late, another meeting with Professor Thornton. Scraps of paper, napkins he had used to write down dates of meetings, notes to himself about the herbarium, Kew Gardens, a new discovery, a new species – one that would make him his name.

Diggy had kept them all and Marian had kept anything and everything that Diggy had written. She knew that it was here – in one of these boxes! She had seen it before. Goddammit! She knew she had seen it before!

In the second to last box, tucked into the corner. She had folded it back into the shape Diggy had made before she had packed it away. Marian slowly unfolded the pleats of the paper airplane and mouthed the words. She watched the tears fall onto the paper. Then she bolted for the door.

The drizzle had started again as she sped into the hospital parking lot and squeezed her small car between two behemoths belonging to the upper echelons of administration. She held the paper tight in her hand, afraid to lose it and, at the same time, afraid to read it again – afraid to confront the man who had written those words.

By the time she arrived on the palliative care ward, the note was damp – partly from the rain, mostly from her worry – and creased from her grip. She grabbed her patient's chart and sat down behind the nurse's desk. She began to search for a clue—a mistake in registration?—a false declaration? – something that she would recognize, something that would make her certain that Karl Crantz was not the man he claimed to be.

There was something odd. The insurance coverage for the patient was completely open ended – fully funded by a drug research firm, Gideon Baldock's company, 'New Age Pharma'. She thought for a moment...Trusteeship.

That's what had been in the papers. 'New Age Pharma' had been placed in trusteeship, taken over by some of Baldock's former associates. And now they fund a casualty of Baldock's expedition.

Why? Did they still think that the seed would be useful – if they could even get a specimen? Or was there something to hide? Or was it because there was something to hide...If they could get a seed? A complication – even a minor complication – that tainted a new discovery could ruin any chance of eventually bringing the new product to market.

Marian continued to flip through the pages of Crantz's chart and barely noticed the flashing red that lit the board at the front of the nurse's station. A nurse stepped forwards and spoke on the telephone. "Could you page the on-call doctor, Dr. MacDermott. For the palliative care ward." She nodded. "No urgency – room 206. It's a 'Do Not Resuscitate' case but he'll have to sign the papers."

"What room did you say?" Marian still held the chart in her hand.

"Dr. Priest!" The nurse took in a deep breath. "You startled me. If I had known you were here-"

"What room did you say?"

"206 – Mr. Crantz." The nurse pursed her lips. "Since you left this afternoon, he's had several episodes of irregular heart beat. In and out of ventricular tachycardia and even a short line of ventricular fibrillation."

She motioned down the hallway. "The nurse with him says that its mostly fibrillation now...It's not a bad way for the poor soul to leave."

"No! Change that order!" Marian grabbed the resuscitation cart and ran down the hallway.

The doctor crashed through the doorway and found the patient staring with unblinking eyes at the ceiling, his gaunt chest heaving shallow, infrequent gasps. Marian pushed the attending nurse away from the patient and yelled, "We'll bring him back!"

"Dr. Priest! This is a 'Do Not Resuscitate'." The nurse shook her head. "It's your order and the patient's decision. You can't-"

"Stand back!" The doctor placed the paddles on Crantz's chest and pressed the trigger.

Karl's chest heaved but his eyes continued their stare at the heavens.

"Again!" Marian slapped the paddles back in place.

"What the hell are you doing, Marian!?" Peter MacDermott was at her side. "He's in v. fib! Let him go!" He grabbed her arm. "Let him go!"

She pushed MacDermott away and triggered the paddles. The body jumped but no response.

"Marian!"

"Stay away, Peter!" Marian held up the two paddles like sword and shield. She turned back to Crantz and sent the shock through her patient again then sat down beside his limp body. She let the paddles fall to the floor and closed her hands over her face.

"Dr. MacDermott." The nurse pulled a strip off the monitor. "Back in sinus rhythm."

"Marian?" MacDermott put a hand on her shoulder. "Why? This...This is completely against protocol. There'll have to be a staff review and-"

"The patient's coming around, doctor."

Karl Crantz moaned and the thickened veins bulged beneath the skin of his arched neck.

Marian stood up and dried her eyes then sat down next to her patient. She kept her gaze fixed on Crantz. "Leave us, Peter...Please. I have to talk to him...Alone."

MacDermott shook his head but did as he was asked.

Crantz moaned again and stared at his doctor through cloudy, confused eyes.

Marian leaned over and stroked her patient's sweaty brow. "Diggy?" She watched the eyes wince shut. "Diggy? I know...Did you think...Did you think that I wouldn't know...The only man I've ever loved?...The only man I've ever loved?...Why didn't you tell me?"

The patient's eyes filled with tears and he covered his face in the bend of his arm.

Marian unfolded the paper she had let fall to the floor. She whispered the words as the monitor whispered back the steady beat of her husband's heart.

> "Death and sweet life
> One sorrow, one bliss..."
> Marian paused and wiped her tears.
> "Each one denied...
> By the Judas Kiss."

"Those are your words, Diggy. Your words that I found in the closet – flown in on a paper airplane ...Just before you left."

Diggy shook his head. "Not my words. Words of a man who did what the Spaniard did...Who did what Baldock did. William Jude Gregor – he left his mother on the mountain and, in those days, he wasn't able to get back in time. But he tried to tell us Marian, to leave a warning..."

"Why-?"

"I couldn't come back to you as an old man, Marian!" Diego wheezed and the veins on his neck swelled then relaxed. "Florentino thought he could help, thought that he could reverse the effects of the seed but...I just kept on growing weaker, sicker... Older."

"We'll find something. I have a friend who researches aging. That's all he does! And he says that a breakthrough-"

The patient tried to smile then shook his head. "Marian...I'm too young to die but...I'm too old...Too old to believe in promises."

Marian lifted her husband's head and gently kissed him on the lips. The wind rocked the window and splashed droplets of fresh rain off the cherry tree and onto the glass.

"She's not a plant." Diggy watched the shadows dance on the windowpane. "Maybe Baldock knows that by now...The Spaniard finally realized it. He finally realized that his Eden – his immortality – was his hell and that...That only death could give him heaven."

Diggy coughed and the fluid rumbled deep in his chest. His lips paled then turned a shade of blue. "Every animal...Every living thing has a way of surviving, Marian...A way of passing on its genes. Even human beings..."

He nodded. "Even human beings have adapted to the most extreme environments – very cold, very dry. But plants...Plants do it so much better than any animal. They can live in the cold, in the heat, in the water, in the desert. Some plants can filter their food from the air and others eat flesh, insects...Like an animal."

The muscles at the base of his neck strained as Diego pulled in each slow breath. "Perhaps that's the dividing line. If it eats anything more than an insect, if it preys on another living being then...Maybe it's not a plant...Not a plant at all."

His body trembled. "No. She's not a plant...Plants use seeds for propagation, to spread themselves but she...She uses her seed to capture her prey...And to drive others away."

Diggy shut his eyes. "Or maybe.....Maybe she's a kind of goddess. Like an ancient Greek goddess living on a mountain.....At the top of the world.....A goddess who takes one man, then another. She keeps him and then....." His voice faded into a whisper.

"But the goddess lives! She always survives!...Maybe forever!"

"No more, Diggy." Marian squeezed his hand. "No more about...About what happened. Just...Just be here. Just be here with me."

The patient's chest heaved and the monitor set off a staccato of heartbeats then slowed. "Florentino said...He said that to die with happiness is...To die with happiness is no death at all...No death at all."

Marian nodded and stared into his eyes.

"That's why I came back, you know." Diego's lips had grown darker and his eyes fainter. "I thought that if I could choose a place to die...If I could choose a place to die, Marian...It would be in your arms."

The doctor lay down next to her patient and wrapped both her arms around his frail body.

The dying storm sighed one last breath then a final gust of wind swept the pebbles of rain off the cherry tree, splashing them against the windowpane. The droplets of spring water flowed slowly at first, twisting across the glass, one drop joining together with the next...Washing away, one by one, the last of the pink blossoms – the beautiful parts – down to the ground.

Epilogue
Springtime –Horstman Glacier, Blackcomb Mountain

The two teenagers swept through the shredded cobs of late season snow, ducking the yellow line that warned of danger and out-of-bounds restriction. It was well past four o'clock and the two were supposed to have started heading downhill over a half-hour before.

But the slopes were always better when they were deserted. And the snow was always better in the restricted areas. That was why the yellow tapes were up, right? To keep the snow fresh for that last run down the mountain.

The first boy tipped his board off the edge of a bluff then shot out into the air – a twenty-foot drop—crashing to the ground with his full weight tucked into a low crouch.

He sprayed the wet snow to a stop and waited for his friend. "Holy shit, man! Look at this!"

The two unstrapped their boards and crawled to the edge of the narrow crevasse.

"I rode this hill last week and this sure wasn't here!" The second youth peered into the depths of the hole. "Over a hundred feet – maybe more. Shit! Maybe the yellow tape doesn't mean 'good snow here'."

They both laughed then the first boy reached down and picked up a pair of smooth stones, two red-stained ovals.

"Topped off in the ice. I must have scraped them up with my board." He rolled one small nut between his gloved fingers then held it up to his nose. "Feels like a rock and smells like a rock but looks like a smootch! Here!" He handed one of the seeds to his friend. "See who can pitch it the farthest."

The two stones sailed through the dying light and landed on the bare rock at the edge of the glacier. For a moment, they both rolled gently across the granite surface then the largest of the two gathered momentum, careened down the slope and dropped into a narrow cavern formed where the mountain had split eons before.

The tiny spore nestled into the damp earth—warm, protected. At last, she had found a home...And now, she could begin to grow.

Robin Rickards was born in Quebec, Canada and lives with his family on the west coast. He works as an orthopaedic surgeon near Vancouver, British Columbia.

ISBN 141202468-4